NIGHTMARES
from Within

JESSICA PRINCE

COPYRIGHT 2013 © JESSICA PRINCE
All rights reserved.

Edited by Becky Johnson at Hot Tree Edits
Formatted by Jovana Shirley at Unforeseen Editing
Cover Design by Meredith Blair at Author's Angels

ISBN-13: 978-1492825364

Visit my Facebook page at
http://www.facebook.com/AuthorJessicaPrince

To Mom,
for always being there no matter what.
This book is for you.

Contents

I can't breathe.

I panic as my lungs beg for air. I reach out to grab hold of the hands around my neck, but nothing is there. I try and try, but all I feel is my own cold, clammy skin. Someone's hands are there; I know it. The grip is so strong that fingernails are digging into my skin, but my hands come in contact with absolutely nothing but my own flesh. My eyes are open, but it serves no purpose. I can't see. Everything is cloaked in darkness so black, that I can't make out what's right in front of my face. My arms are thrashing now, desperate to escape the vise-like grasp, but still...nothing's there.

What's happening to me?

My body trembles and sweat breaks out across my forehead. I can feel my life slowly slipping away, and I know instinctively that I'm going to die here. I have no idea where I am. I just know I don't want to die this way...alone. As I slip further and further toward unconsciousness, the fear of dying overwhelms me. Tears rain down my cheeks. I reach for my neck one last time, desperately trying to free myself from the constricting grip, but there's nothing there.

I'm losing hope and fading fast.

That's when I hear it. A dark, gravely laugh. If there was ever a sound that could be described as pure evil, it's that laugh. "Tell me you love me."

That voice. I know that voice. I wrack my brain, quickly trying to remember its source, but I'm so far gone that I can't think. I should know who this voice...this man is. Every fiber in my body is screaming that I know him.

But how?

"Tell me you love me and I'll let you go."

He's lying. I'm going to die whether I say it or not, but I have to try. I can't just give up. Summoning my strength, I force out the words, "I love you." It's the last breath in my body and I know I've just wasted it. Now, I have nothing left.

The voice before me grows more menacing as he yells, "I don't believe you!" I've never felt so terrified, and I know the end is moments away.

I shot up in bed screaming, "Nooo!" I sucked in so much air, I thought my chest would explode. My hair and clothes were drenched in sweat, as were the sheets tangled all around my legs. The nightmares that had just started a few months ago were gradually getting worse. This particular dream had been plaguing me for weeks and was gradually becoming more realistic. As I brushed the hair off my face, I knew in that moment, it was time for a higher dosage of medication. I couldn't stand the idea of having to see Dr. Kinsley again, but that was clearly what I needed. It made sense. I'd been on the same dosage since I was fifteen. Now, at twenty-three, it was obvious the meds weren't doing the job they were supposed to. It was time to up them.

I glanced at the red numbers on my alarm clock. 3:30 a.m. *Just fucking perfect.*

I had too much adrenaline pumping through my body, and as if that wasn't enough, the fact that I was afraid to close my eyes just guaranteed that I'd be living off coffee for another day.

I rubbed my hands roughly over my face and flung my legs over the side of the bed. If I wasn't going to be able to sleep, I might as well do one of the only things that helped expel the restless energy coursing through my veins.

Exercise.

Typically, I was a fan of yoga. It helped clear all of the haunting pictures that ran through my mind on a non-stop reel. I knew yoga wasn't going to cut it this time. I didn't need to relax this time; I needed to pound the energy into the concrete. I could still feel the hands on my neck, and I needed to do something that would chase the memories from my mind.

I headed for the bathroom and brushed my teeth before throwing on a pair of running shorts and a tank top. I laced up my battered running shoes, strapped my iPod to my arm and headed out the door.

I knew that running through the streets of Seattle at 3:45 in the morning wasn't the smartest thing to do—especially when there was someone out there targeting young women—but honestly, I was less afraid of the serial killer the media had dubbed "The Poet" than I was my own nightmare. Apparently years of hallucinations desensitized me to the horrors of the world. Why worry about the monsters on the streets when it was the monsters in my head that tormented me daily?

I rode the elevator down from my Harbor Steps apartment to the ornate marble lobby. I hoped to make it through the glass doors and out onto First Street uninterrupted, but on top of being crazy, I also had the worst luck in the world.

"Miss Taylor…"

I turned to see the doorman on duty watching me with concern etched on his pudgy, red face. His bushy, silver eyebrows were pulled down and frown lines were etched deeply around his eyes. "Please, it's not safe for you out there. Can't you use one of the treadmills in the gym?"

It was an argument we had routinely over the past several months…ever since the nightmares began plaguing my sleep. Gary was a sweet, old man who I'd come to care for in my time at Harbor Steps. He was one of the very few people I interacted with by choice.

"Gary, I've told you, I'm perfectly fine out there. You have nothing to be concerned about. And for Christ's sake, please stop calling me *Miss*. You have kids older than me."

He plastered a stern expression on his face and huffed, "I don't like it, Taylor. Please use the gym."

I rolled my shoulders, trying to ease some of the tension. I appreciated his concern, but I couldn't explain to him why I needed to run outside. Not only did I need the fresh air, I needed to see the buildings and feel the city around me. It wasn't only the run that did the trick. Being stuck in a stale gym with the smell of rubber flooring and mirrors from wall-to-wall never allowed the escape I needed to expel the images I'd seen.

If I tried to explain to him what I was desperately trying to forget, he'd look at me just like everyone else back home did. Like I needed to be locked up, away from the rest of the world. Call me crazy, but after spending my entire life keeping people at a distance, the last thing I wanted was for one of the few I'd actually let in, to think of me the way *they* did.

"Gary, if I'm not back in an hour, you have my permission to call the cops," I tried to joke.

But it was clear he didn't find me funny at all when he replied, "They found another girl last night, Taylor. She was only a year older than you. You don't know how dangerous it is out on those streets in the dark."

If he only knew how wrong he was. I knew exactly how dangerous they were.

I couldn't stand around talking with him anymore, because I knew I was minutes from a panic attack. I had to get out of that lobby before I lost it.

"I'm going, Gary. I'll be back. I promise." Before he could protest further, I was out the door, taking a left down First Street and heading in the direction of Pike Place Market. Everything would still be closed at this hour, but it was a route that I knew by heart. So, I just let my legs carry me away as Nine Inch Nails blared through my ear buds. *Every Day Is Exactly the Same* was the theme song for my life; wake up, grab coffee from the shop down the street, head to work and then go home. It was routine. It might seem boring to most, but keeping a routine was one of the only things that helped me hold on to what little sanity I had left. If I deviated from the schedule I set for myself, I put myself at risk for more hallucinations, and that meant more panic attacks.

Keeping things the same kept me safe.

As Trent Reznor's voice faded and the opening chords of Red's *Lie to Me* picked up, I turned right off First and onto Pike Street. I kept going until my legs felt like they couldn't hold my weight any longer. I made the familiar turns through downtown Seattle, pushing through the cramp that began throbbing in my side. Pushing through the exhaustion pulsing in every muscle. I'd made sure my iPod was set to my "running" playlist before leaving my apartment, so when *Chalk Outline* by Three Days Grace started playing, I knew I was nearing the end of my run.

I was almost sad to see my apartment building looming in the distance. I needed just a few more miles to get myself straight, but running any farther meant changing my precious routine.

I slowed to a walk a few yards from the building and worked to get my heart rate under control. By the time I pushed through the glass doors, the endorphins had kicked in and I felt as close to normal as was possible for me.

When Gary looked up from the novel he was reading with a scowl on his face, a smile crept across my lips. He typically reminded me of a short-haired Santa Claus without the beard, but when he pouted, he reminded me of Walter Matthau from *Grumpy Old Men.*

"See, I'm back and still in one piece," I said, as I swiped the beads of sweat from my forehead.

"You're going to send me into an early grave, Miss Taylor," he replied.

I rested my arms on the cool granite counter top and leaned over to see his book. "Which one are you reading now?" I asked.

I think one of the reasons he and I got along as well as we did was because Gary was also a creature of habit. If it wasn't a Stephen King novel, Gary wouldn't read it. And once Gary read them all, he'd just start over again. He said King had enough books out there that by the time he started over, he'd already forgotten what happened in the ones he'd read before.

"*The Dark Half,*" he grumbled.

"That's a good one," I said with a sincere smile. It was just too easy to love Gary.

"That's why I'm reading it," he bit back harshly, his tone of voice letting me know that he was still upset with me. He might have still been angry, but I had a trick up my sleeve to get myself back on his good side.

"You know, since I woke up early enough, I was planning on making some cinnamon streusel muffins before I headed to work, but…if you're still mad at me, I guess I shouldn't bother."

I turned and headed toward the elevators. I only made it a few steps when I heard him clear his throat behind me. "Well, I'm not *that* mad, Miss Taylor." I knew I'd get him with the promise of baked goods. I turned and he continued, "I just look at you as one of my own." His honesty was like a shot through the heart. No one had ever cared about my well-being, so having this brusque old man openly worry about me was something I wasn't accustomed to.

I walked back to him and placed my hands on his stubbly cheeks. "I know, Gary. That's why I tolerate you calling me *Miss* all the time, even after I've asked you not to…repeatedly."

He graced me with a happy chuckle.

"I'm thankful I met you, Gary," I said, then I headed back to my apartment to shower and make his muffins.

I made the usual walk from the coffee shop to Benny's Diner with my head down, making sure I didn't make eye contact with any of the pedestrians as they passed me on the sidewalk. I'd been waitressing at Benny's for the past five years and I felt it gave me just the right amount of human interaction to call myself normal, but I didn't want to push my nonexistent luck any further than that. I could only avoid so much in one day. So I kept my head down and rarely ever interacted with the strangers I passed.

I loved Seattle, but I didn't get to truly appreciate everything around me in the daytime. Too many people wandering around meant I was way more susceptible to those visions that plagued me.

After my morning stop at the coffee shop around the corner from my apartment, it was six o'clock. I pushed through the doors of the diner a half hour early so I headed straight for the office in the back to drop off my purse and began prepping myself for the morning rush.

"Good morning, Doll Face," Benny called from behind the serving window.

"Morning, Benny." My boss, the owner of the diner was another on my short list of who I considered my friend. If I had to guess, Benny was somewhere in her mid-to-late fifties. Her chestnut colored hair was sprinkled with gray and her light brown skin showed signs of wrinkles around her eyes and mouth. The smile lines on her face proved what I already knew, that Benny was one of the most caring, loving women in the world. She barely hit five feet but her short, round stature didn't mask the fact that she could be tough as nails when it was necessary.

She poured all of her heart and soul into opening this diner after she divorced her abusive husband fifteen years ago. Benny once admitted to me that, although she always wanted kids, she was thankful not to have anything that tied her to her ex-husband. She claimed that when I wandered in five years ago desperate for a job, she took one look at me and all of her maternal instincts just sprang to life. After years of having two parents that looked at me like I was a freak of nature, it was nice to have Gary and Benny treat me like I was family.

It took a while to get used to them and I spent my first year trying to push them away. I'd spent so long trying not to connect with other people, but they gave me no choice and simply refused to let me keep them out of my life. They saw through my hardened exterior to the scared teenager I really was, and they beat at the walls I'd put up around myself until there was nothing left. I loved the both of them so much, that every night I prayed to a God I wasn't sure I believed in and gave thanks for allowing them to stay in my life.

I downed the last of my white chocolate mocha and headed straight for the coffee maker to pour myself a huge cup. There was no chance of me making it through the day without at least three cups in my system. I was a caffeine addict on a regular day, but when you added no sleep into the mix, coffee went from being something I enjoyed, to an absolute necessity.

"Child, you look like death warmed over," Benny pointed out, as she made her way over to me. I could see the concern etched onto her face and it was the last thing I wanted to deal with.

"Thanks, Benny. It gives me the warm fuzzies to know you think I look so good."

"You had another nightmare didn't you?" she asked as her eyes raked over my face, ignoring my sarcastic attempt at derailing a conversation I didn't want to have with her.

I'd made the mistake of letting it slip when the nightmares first started a few months back. I was so scared after that first night, that when I came into work, I couldn't hold it in. I poured everything out for Benny and actually allowed her to comfort me. I'd been dealing with horrifying hallucinations since childhood, but nightmares were something completely different. It was almost as if the visions were following me into my sleep, and I had no idea how to make them stop.

I placed the glass carafe back down and took a huge gulp from my cup, letting the warmth fill my body and put me at ease...temporarily. "Yeah," I finally relented. "Around 3:30."

She came up to me and took my face in her hands. "Sweetheart, you have bags under your eyes big enough to carry all that weight I know you currently keep on your shoulders. I'm worried about you."

I took a small step back in order to break the physical contact. I loved Benny, but overt displays of affection still made me uncomfortable. It was just one of the many things I was trying to work through. I'd gotten better at accepting people touching me over the years, but I was only able to tolerate it for short periods of time. As a teenager, I'd discovered that any contact longer than a few seconds made the things I was forced to see even stronger.

I gave her a weak smile and tried to placate her. "I'm okay, Benny. I promise."

The corners of her mouth dipped into a frown. "You're not okay, Taylor, you look exhausted. Why don't you take the day off and go home? You need some sleep."

I couldn't sleep. Sleeping only led to more nightmares.

I couldn't admit to Benny that I was too scared to go back to sleep; she'd only worry more. I hadn't missed a day of work in five years and the mere thought of straying from the comforts of my routine caused anxiety to build until my hands started to shake.

"I'm fine, really," I lied. "I'm just going to throw myself into work and get my mind straight, that's all." I needed her to let me stay. I needed the hours on my feet, rushing around and waiting on people to keep me occupied. The constant bustle of the diner prevented me from being sucked into the horrors of my own mind. Being on my feet all day long, running back and forth to serve the diners that came through helped in exhausting me to the point where I could hopefully pass out into a dreamless sleep when I got home.

If I didn't keep myself busy constantly I would start to remember…and the last thing I wanted was to remember. From the moment I woke up, until the moment I went to bed, I made sure I had something to fill every hour of my day. If I was at home I was doing yoga, running, baking, or cleaning my already immaculate apartment. There always had to be something. Sleep was the only time my brain was allowed to shut down. I used to cherish sleep. I could escape the things I saw when I slept. Now sleep was becoming my enemy. If I didn't get in to see Dr. Kinsley soon, the fraying rope that somehow managed to tether me to reality was at risk of snapping completely.

Benny watched me closely for several more seconds, and it almost felt as though she could see what I was thinking. I held my breath as I waited for her to say something. "All right," she finally conceded, and I was able to breathe again. "If you think it's what's best, fine. But if you start to feel like you need to leave, you just let me know, okay?"

"Promise," I replied a little too quickly. Benny's smile lines were gone as concern marred her expression. She and I both knew I wouldn't be leaving until my shift was over.

As the morning wore on, and the diners started packing in, I reveled in the organized chaos. It was exactly what I needed. I even found myself shooting small smiles at some of the customers here and there which was rare. I'd just finished serving one of my tables when I looked up and noticed a man sitting alone in my section.

"Hey Taylor, I just sat someone at seven." I turned my attention away from the man to Cassie, Benny's hostess and newest hire. If I had to guess, I'd say she was around my age. Cassie was the stereotypical model type with long, glossy brown hair, even longer legs and a bubbly personality. I didn't know her all that well, but the few times we'd worked together, I got the sense she was a genuinely good person. Maybe I'd make the effort to get to know her a little better. It wasn't like I had friends coming out of the woodwork, so I certainly had room to spare.

"Thanks, Cass."

"You're so lucky," she whispered with a smile that looked like she was letting me in on a secret. "I'd die for a piece like that." She tilted her head in the direction of table seven.

I tilted my head in confusion. "What are you talking about?"

Her forehead wrinkled and her eyes narrowed before asking, "You mean you don't know him? He specifically asked to be seated in your section. I thought you two might have a thing?"

I looked at the man in question, studying him hard for any signs that I may have known who he was. I felt a sense of recognition, but I couldn't place him. There was something niggling in the back of my mind telling me I knew him.

"Well," Cassie stated, directing my attention back to her. "Maybe you have an admirer." She looked at the man, looked back at me, and then she winked. "Could be worse, you know. I wouldn't kick him out of my bed."

I let out a laugh as she headed back to the hostess stand, and I made my way to table seven. "Good morning," I greeted. "What can I getcha?"

I had my eyes on my order pad, but they instantly shot up to meet his when he replied, "Good morning to you, Taylor." He said my name like he'd spoken it a million times before. He must have seen the shock on my face, because he grinned and pointed to my red Benny's Diner t-shirt.

"Your name tag says Taylor. That is your name, isn't it?"

His question sounded almost accusatory, like he knew something he wasn't supposed to. I'd never seen this man before. It wasn't possible for him to know Taylor wasn't the name I'd been born with.

"Um…yeah," I responded carefully.

The grin on his face morphed into a full on smile, and I could see what Cassie had been talking about. He was extremely handsome. His jet-black hair was a few inches too long and flopped over his forehead, but it accentuated his crystal blue eyes perfectly. I felt a strong pull as I looked into them. I didn't know how long I stood there staring into those strange eyes but I was yanked back into reality when he cleared his throat and gave a little chuckle.

Embarrassed at being caught staring, heat started to creep up my neck and I had no doubt my cheeks were bright pink. My blush was the curse of having such a fair complexion. A complexion I got from my Irish mother. It was one of the only things I got from her. Everything else about me favored my father. Dark, wavy brown hair and light brown eyes. I had no doubt my darker features combined with my pale skin made the circles under my eyes - that Benny was concerned about - even more pronounced.

"I'm Daniel," the man said as he held out his hand in an introduction.

I glanced down, knowing he was waiting for me to shake his hand and I couldn't stop the pang that went through me at the thought of touching him. I might not like to touch people, but in my line of work, it was sometimes necessary. I didn't want to come off rude and risk getting a lousy tip just because of my own idiosyncrasies.

I placed my hand in his and instantly regretted it. Visions from my childhood shot through my head like a movie on fast forward. I caught glimpses of memories that I wanted to lock in a vault and never remember again, but they wouldn't stop. They all came flooding back in Technicolor, but something was terribly wrong. The memories that flashed through my head were different. I was seeing things that I remembered, but they weren't from *my* memories. They were *his*. I snatched my hand back like I'd been burned, and looked at the man named Daniel through wide, horrified eyes.

"What the hell was that?" I asked in a whisper as I lifted a shaky hand to wipe away the beads of perspiration that had formed on my brow. "Do I know you?"

His knowing smile caused ice to run through my veins. "What do you think?"

At the horrifying memories the flashes from my past had caused, a wave of nausea rolled through my stomach and I had to clamp a hand over my mouth to keep from throwing up all over the table. I ran through the crowded diner and made it to the bathroom just in time to lose my breakfast in the toilet.

My stomach lurched until there was nothing left. Once I was finished, I pulled toilet paper off the roll to wipe my mouth and sat back against the metal door of the stall. The coolness against my skin helped, and eventually, I was able to pull myself up and walk to the sink to rinse that acrid taste from my mouth.

As I swished the water around, the bathroom door flew open and Cassie came rushing over to me. "Ohmigod Taylor, are you okay?"

I rested my palms on the edge of the counter and dropped my head. "Did everyone see me run in here?" Benny was going to send me home for sure now. I just knew it.

"I don't think so."

Thank God.

"The only reason I noticed was because I was watching you and the hottie. You shook his hand then turned white as a damn ghost before you booked it in here. Are you all right? What happened?"

I needed to come up with something fast. It couldn't be anything catching that would risk me being sent home before my shift ended, so I went with the first thing that popped in my head. "Low blood sugar, I think." It was a lame excuse, but when I chanced a look at Cassie's face, I could see she'd bought it. "I went for a run this morning and came to work without eating breakfast. I guess my body just bottomed out on me."

She reached up and began to pat my back soothingly. I tried to mask the instinctive flinch I felt anytime someone touched me with a shiver and I must have been successful because she didn't remove her hand right away. "I have an

unopened toothbrush in my purse. You want me to go get it?"
Her kindness was almost too much on my frayed nerves, but I
had to get the taste out of my mouth before it caused me to
puke again.

"That would be great. Thank you."

She smiled brightly. "Sure thing. Hang tight and I'll be
right back."

Once I was alone in the bathroom, I looked in the mirror
and studied my reflection. I felt as if the woman I was looking
at was a total stranger to me. If you looked past the tired eyes
you'd see a woman that most people would consider to be
pretty. Light brown eyes, that from a distance, looked almost
copper and hair that fell in waves down the length of my back
almost to my waist. I only stood at 5'3, but years of yoga and
running kept my muscles long and lean. Combined with the
generous curves I had thanks to my father's family, I had a
pretty decent figure.

But I already knew from experience that appearances
didn't stand for anything. For all the pretty on the outside I
was a dark and ugly mess on the inside. For every person that
asked 'how is that young girl single?' I'd think to myself 'who
in their right mind would want to deal with all my crazy?'

I was a giant ball of neuroses wrapped in a pretty little
package.

"Here you go. Oral B, the brand most dentists use."

I looked up at Cassie and gave her a small smile that didn't
quite reach my eyes. "Thank you for this," I replied softly,
pointing at the toothbrush.

"No problem. I haven't been here long and you've always
been nice to me, so I wanted to do something nice for you in
return." The sincerity in her voice caused a crack in my
protective armor. She knew there was something strange about
me, everyone I spent more than a few minutes with knew, but
that didn't seem to matter to her. That caused my smile to
become more genuine and I felt myself warming up to her.

Cassie returned my smile and flashed her pearly whites.

She leaned against the sink next to me as I brushed my teeth, and strangely, it didn't feel uncomfortable having her around me. I knew she stayed for no other reason than to make sure I was okay. Because of that alone, I couldn't have stopped my growing respect for her even if I wanted to. "You okay to go back out there?" she asked once I'd finished and was wiping my mouth. I thought about the man at table seven and cringed.

Daniel.

"Is he still out there?" There was no way of masking the quiver in my voice. Something about him opened up memories I didn't want to remember.

"Yeah. But I can get one of the other girls to take that table if you want. Or I can even ask him to leave if you're not comfortable with him being here."

The thought of interacting with him again wasn't exactly at the top of my list, but my gut told me that this man had answers to questions I'd carried with me most of my life. I *needed* answers.

"It's okay, Cassie. I'll be out in just a minute."

"Everything okay?" Daniel asked once I was standing in front of his table again. The level of concern shining in his bright blue eyes wasn't something you'd expect from a person you just met.

I wasn't sure how to ask him all the questions that were flying around in my head so I just nodded and pulled the order pad from my apron. I was a coward. "Yeah, I'm good. Are you ready to order?"

He laced his fingers together and rested his arms on the table. His eyes bore into mine as he studied every contour of my face. "You look tired, Taylor." From the slightly amused tone of his voice and the small grin on his lips I got the distinct impression that he was baiting me. "Not getting much sleep? Let me guess...nightmares?"

The order pad and pen slipped from my hands. The tiny hairs on my arms stood on end. His knowing expression never wavered as shock spread through every cell in my body. It could have been a generic question asked by anyone— everyone had nightmares—but there was knowledge in his eyes, something that shone through telling me that he wasn't just guessing. He knew.

"Who are you?" I finally managed to ask, though I whispered so quietly I was afraid he didn't hear me.

One side of his mouth twitched, and I had to quell the deep desire to slap the smile off his face. "I told you, my name's Daniel."

He wanted to play games and I wasn't in the mood at all. I hadn't had a good night's sleep in forever; I was functioning solely on coffee, Red Bull, and determination, and I had just finished turning my stomach inside out.

I. Was. Not. In. The. Mood.

I put my clenched fists on the table and leaned in so that only he could hear me. "Cut the shit, *Daniel*. You know what I mean. Why do I feel like I know you and what the fuck did you do to me when you shook my hand? And *don't you dare* act like you don't know what I'm talking about, or I swear to God, I'll call the cops and tell them I have a creepy-ass stalker that won't leave me alone. I don't give a damn how good looking you are." I straightened and placed my hands on my hips, trying my hardest to look intimidating even though I was visibly trembling.

He remained silent for several seconds before responding. "I thought you didn't believe in God."

What the fuck?

"That's it, I'm done. I'm calling the cops." I spun on my heels as fast as I could and started toward the office in the back. The next sentence out of his mouth froze me in place.

"Come back, Lydia."

The sound of him saying my name—my *real* name—caused panic. My heart started beating so hard I was certain the people at the other end of the diner could hear it.

When I slowly turned back around, the knowing smirk he previously wore on his face was gone. He almost looked like he felt sorry.

"How do you know my name?"

He could see the hesitance in my body. His shoulders lifted in a shrug and he let out a deep sigh before standing to remove his wallet from the back pocket of his jeans. "We can't discuss this here," he responded. "But when you're ready to know the truth, I'm the one who has the answers."

He dropped a twenty on the table for a meal he didn't even order and started for the door. All of the sudden, desperation surged through me. I needed to know what he knew. "Wait," I blurted out as I ran to him and grabbed hold of his arm. People in the diner were staring at the interaction between me and Daniel, but I didn't care. "Answers to what?"

He placed his warm palm over the hand that was gripping his arm and gave it a reassuring pat. "You aren't ready yet, but trust me, you will be soon. I will tell you this though, if you'd just stop fighting your gift and opened yourself up to it, maybe the nightmares would end." His voice dropped low as he whispered, "See you soon Taylor."

And then he was gone, leaving me reeling and freaked the *fuck* out.

//

"What's wrong, Taylor? You look like you've seen a ghost," Benny asked as she placed a hand on my forehead like she was checking for a fever.

I don't know what I just saw.

I gave my head a hard shake, trying to remove the exchange with Daniel but it was no use. I was certain I'd never seen him before but the feeling of familiarity had been imprinted on my brain.

I inhaled a cleansing breath and tried to slow my heart down as I exhaled. I pasted on a cheerful smile and turned to Benny. "I just thought I saw someone I knew, but I was wrong."

If she didn't believe me, she thankfully didn't push it any further. I went back to waiting tables and pushed Daniel into the far recesses of my mind. That was where I kept everything I didn't want to deal with in my life. He was wrong about one thing though. I didn't care how badly I wanted answers, I never planned to see him again.

//

"Welcome to Benny's, gentlemen. What can I get you?" I managed to fake my way through the breakfast rush and by lunch I was finally feeling a little better.

"You mean besides your number?" Guy One asked. I lifted my head from my order pad to look at the man who'd just hit on me. It wasn't like I never got hit on; I'd had my fair share of customers come on to me over the years, but I didn't think I'd ever get used to it. Because of the things I saw and tried to hide from the outside world, I couldn't allow myself the comfort of a relationship. I just had too many other things I had to worry about. Adding a boyfriend to the mix wasn't something I was interested in.

And Guy One wasn't going to be changing my mind any time soon.

As if the muffin top hanging over his belt and stretching the buttons on his shirt to an insulting level wasn't enough of a turn off, his rancid onion breath and the leftover food stuck in his teeth from breakfast did him in.

"Sorry, sir. I'm married." The lie rolled off my tongue just as easily as it always did.

"Well, I didn't see a ring on your pretty little finger. Figured you were on the market."

I might not have been married, but I was definitely *off* the market.

"Hazards of the job," I replied with a sweet smile. "Don't want to risk losing it." I turned my attention from Stank Breath to his friend to take his order and was instantly struck speechless. The most gorgeous hazel eyes I'd ever seen were smiling back at me. I somehow managed to pull my focus from his eyes and trailed over the rest of his face. His nose was slightly crooked, like it had been broken earlier in his life, and a light dusting of blond stubble covered his strong, square jaw. His dirty-blond hair was standing up like he'd been running his hands through it all day and the look was seriously working for him. A large part of me wanted to reach over and run my hands through the shiny strands just to see if they felt as silky as they looked, but I managed to refrain. When he laughed my eyes zoomed down to his mouth and I noticed his perfect, white teeth outlined by the most amazing, full lips.

Lips meant for kissing.

Lips meant to do serious damage to a woman's self-control.

To *my* self control.

I'd never reacted to a man before the way I did this guy and the intensity of it was startling. I shouldn't be feeling the way I was. I couldn't. It was detrimental to my sanity.

I quickly averted my gaze to the tabletop in front of me and cleared my throat uncomfortably.

"Stevens, leave the poor woman alone. I'm sure her standards are a lot higher than a piece of shit like you." The smile on his face and chuckle in his voice showed that he was just giving his friend a hard time, but the deep timber of his voice rumbled through me and warmed me from the inside out.

"Ah, her loss," Stevens, formerly-known-as-Stank-Breath replied. "I gotta take a piss. Get me the Reuben, would ya?"

I scribbled his order down as he walked away from the table, making sure to keep my eyes on the pad in front of me instead of on the man with the beautiful eyes.

"Sorry about him. He was dropped on his head as an infant."

I couldn't stop the blush from creeping up my neck as he spoke to me in that rich, decadent voice.

"More than once?" I asked.

He gifted me with the most melodic laugh I'd ever heard. I wanted to record that sound and play it over and over every night until I fell asleep with it imprinted in my mind.

"Yeah. I'm pretty sure it was an everyday occurrence."

I reached up and fiddled with the locket at the base of my neck, a habit I'd had since I was a child. Any time I felt uncomfortable I would grab onto the locket my grandmother passed down to me on my seventh birthday. Granny was the only family member that I remember ever feeling close to. Something about touching the locket soothed me and made me feel grounded.

We both stayed quiet for what felt like an eternity, before he finally broke the silence. "You aren't really married, are you?" He made it sound like a statement. "Please tell me a woman as beautiful as yourself isn't already taken, because if that's the case, I'm giving up on humanity as a whole."

How could I even respond to that? I knew my eyes were the size of golf balls and the small blush had turned into a full blown reddish purple. "Um. Uh…" I stuttered. "I'm just going to go put in your order."

I started to scurry off to the kitchen when his voice stopped me. "But I haven't ordered anything."

I squeezed my eyes shut in embarrassment and turned around. "Shit. I'm so sorry." I rushed to pull my pad and pen out of my apron and managed to drop them both on the ground as I fumbled around.

I bent to pick them up at the same time he did, but he got there first. "Easy there, Crimson." I heard the smile in his voice and when I stood back up, I was surprised to find his eyes were trained on my face as opposed to my chest.

"Crimson?" I had to ask. I normally took orders and interacted with customers only as much as was absolutely necessary, but there was something about him that made me *want* to stay. Made me want to talk to him more just to hear his voice.

"Yeah. Every time you get nervous or embarrassed you turn bright red. It's actually really cute."

And there went the blush again.

"See! Like right now. Do I make you nervous, Crimson?"

He lowered his voice and the deep register caused a tingle down in my belly. Oh God. This man was doing horrible things to my non-existent libido.

I had to put a stop to it.

"My name's Taylor, not Crimson, and no, you don't make me nervous. Now if you don't mind, I have other tables I need to take care of, so can you just give me your order so I can go about my job and take care of my other customers?"

I'd never felt worse shooting a man down, but it had to be done. I wasn't made for relationships. I was too damaged.

Those full lips went into a tight, straight line and his eyebrows dipped down in a frown. I missed his smile as soon as it was gone. "I'm sorry. I didn't mean to insult you." He opened his menu and started looking through it quickly. I couldn't walk away from his table with him thinking he'd insulted me. I knew it was dangerous and stupid, but I had an insane need to see that smile on his face again.

I did something so completely out of character that it startled me just as much as it did him. I placed my small hand down over his larger one and smiled down at him. "You didn't insult me," I said softly. "It's just been a long day. I'm sorry for being so rude."

At that moment, it was as if an electric current moved from his hand to mine, sending a small jolt through my body. I looked at his face and saw that his mouth was slightly open and his eyes were a little wider than before. He felt it too.

He cleared his throat and gave his head a little shake. "Um...I'll take the turkey club."

I scribbled his order down and gave him another shy grin. "Got it. I'll put your order in now."

I turned to walk away, but was stopped again when he gently put his hand on my forearm. The current came back as soon as he touched me.

"I'm Jordan. It's nice to meet you, Taylor," He said with a wide grin. Something about that smile heated me from the inside out.

"Nice to meet you too, Jordan," I replied shyly.

He softly ran his fingers down my forearm before removing his hand completely and goose bumps broke out across my skin. "You aren't going to tell me if you're really married, are you?"

I let out a tiny laugh and shook my head. "No."

"No you won't tell me, or no, you aren't married?"

I threw my head back and released the first real laugh I'd had in ages. I was starting to feel like a different person; a little lighter and more carefree. "No I won't tell you."

Am I flirting? Shit. I can't do this. I cannot flirt with this guy!

He opened his mouth to respond, but his friend took that moment to return from the bathroom. "Whew! Man, I had to piss like a Russian race horse!" he announced loudly.

I took that as my cue to make my escape from Jordan and his intoxicating voice.

The rest of the lunch rush went by without anymore flirting or blushing on my part, but that didn't mean I couldn't feel the constant burn of Jordan's eyes on me as I moved through the diner.

His friend did a damn good job of being the perfect buffer between us and I was both grateful and irritated all at the same time. I knew the interaction between me and Jordan wasn't safe, but I couldn't stop myself from wanting that feeling of being free from my personal hell whenever he talked to me.

When they stood to leave a small part of me broke as I watched him walk out the door. He made me feel things I'd never experienced before, things I didn't know were even possible for me to feel. I was sad that he was gone but thankful for the few minutes I'd had with him.

I went to clear the table and that was when I saw it.

A small piece of paper the size of a business card. The handwriting was damn near illegible but I still managed to make out what it said.

Crimson,

It was an absolute pleasure meeting you. I hope to see your beautiful face again soon, but until then, I'll settle for your equally beautiful voice.

I turned the card over and saw that he'd scrawled his number on the back of it.

I knew I wasn't going to call him. I didn't have the luxury of entertaining thoughts about having a relationship, but that didn't mean I couldn't enjoy gaining the attention of an attractive man. A huge smile slowly spread across my face and there was no way of removing it as I worked the rest of my shift. It felt like things were finally looking up.

"I've never seen you smile so much in all the years I've know you, Doll. It wouldn't happen to be because of that tall, blond sex-on-a-stick that was in here during lunch, would it?"

I should have known better than to think Benny would let my change in demeanor slide without drawing attention to it. And just as I expected, a lot of the other staff had to join in on her good-natured ribbing. "I don't know what you're talking about," I said, keeping my head lowered as I wiped down tables and began placing chairs on top. I blushed whenever I thought of Jordan, which just reminded me of our entire encounter. That in turn caused me to blush even harder. It was a vicious cycle.

"What were you reading when Blondie left earlier?" one of the other waitresses asked. "I thought you were gonna break your face, smiling that wide." Everyone around me laughed and I couldn't help but join in. I hadn't felt so good in…well…ever, actually. I'd never felt a part of something the way I did just then, standing around being teased about a guy.

"I know something you don't know," Cassie sing-songed from behind me.

We all looked her way and waited for her to spill. "A certain hot blond stopped by the hostess stand on his way out and asked for a certain waitress's phone number."

My skin went damp and the blush disappeared leaving me paler than normal. Things just changed drastically in the blink of an eye.

I let myself appreciate having a handsome man who I was attracted to hit on me, but I never intended to follow through with anything. There was too much risk, too much fear. I just wanted to feel alive for a little while and now that was gone. If he had my number and called to ask me out would I actually be able to turn him down? Could I resist that sinful voice and make the decision I knew was the safest for me?

Shit!

Cassie must have noticed how panic-stricken I'd become because she put both hands on my shoulders and hunched down to eye level. "Calm down, Taylor. I didn't give it to him."

I let out a huge sigh of relief and my entire body slumped as the tension seeped away.

But then she burst my bubble almost as quickly as she'd inflated it. "But I don't think that's going to stop him; he seemed pretty determined."

Benny came up beside me and bumped my shoulder playfully. "I bet he's back in here before you know it."

She and Cassie were both smiling like that was a good thing and I couldn't expect them to understand why it wasn't.

I stopped at the little corner store on my way home to grab a sandwich for a late dinner and something caught my attention as I stood at the checkout line.

THE POET CLAIMS ANOTHER VICTIM.

I wasn't sure why, but that bold font headline pulled me in and I found myself dropping the copy of The Seattle Times on the counter next to my dinner for the cashier to ring up.

As I walked down the street toward my apartment I started to read the article that warranted front-page news.

> *Police have confirmed that the body of Sylvia Garcia, the twenty year old Seattle resident that was found in SoDo earlier this week, was a victim of the killer people are referring to as The Poet.*

Deputy Chief Walters is not answering any questions related to the poem left at the scene at this time, but in a press conference late yesterday evening, he verified that one was found. There is no word yet on whether police are classifying this man as a serial killer, but sources say that there have been no suspects or persons of interest so far.

The only information being given in this case is that the sites where the women's bodies have been located were not where the murders occurred.

This is the third confirmed killing in four months. On February 16, the body of eighteen year old Alicia Gilbert was found by pedestrians in Pioneer Square; just weeks later, on April 2, twenty-two year old Marissa Waters' body was found by a dock worker near Coleman Dock, Pier 52.

State officials are urging all females between the ages of seventeen and twenty-five to be conscious of their surroundings at all times.

I was so engrossed in the article that before I realized it, I was walking up the steps of my apartment building. As I pushed through the doors, Gary raised his head and quickly noticed the newspaper clutched tightly in my hands.

"Miss Taylor, you shouldn't be reading about that. It'll give you nightmares for weeks."

If you only knew. I thought.

The article wasn't going to be the cause of the nightmares, but it certainly hadn't helped to read about those poor young women. I turned my attention from the paper to Gary. "It's okay. I just feel awful for these women's families."

He nodded in agreement. "Me too. Now do you understand why I just about have a heart attack every time you go jogging at three in the morning? Imagine how your parents would feel if they found out anything bad happened to you."

I didn't bother telling him that my parents didn't have the time or desire to worry about my safety. They didn't even know or care where I was. I moved away from Connecticut and that perfect little country club, politically-endorsed Hell, clear across the country as soon as I was able to. They probably threw a party to celebrate being rid of the embarrassment that had been holding them back for eighteen years. The only thing that my folks did for me was allow me access to my trust fund the second I graduated high school. With that and the hefty checks their accountant deposited in my bank account each month to keep me away, I had plenty of money and didn't really need to work.

But like I said, the distraction was a necessity.

I spoke over my shoulder as I made my way to the elevator. "Tell you what, Gary, I'll start running on the treadmills in the gym, but you have to promise to stop calling me Miss."

He placed his hand over his heart like I'd just granted him a lifelong wish. "You've got yourself a deal, Taylor," he replied with a wink.

I'd just pushed the key into the lock when the tell-tale ache started at the base of my skull.

"Oh God, not again." I didn't want this. I didn't want to see how another person was going to die. If it was a gift, I wanted the giver to take it the fuck back! If it was a curse I didn't know what I'd ever done that was so bad to warrant such an awful punishment.

I managed to get my door open just as the sharp, blinding pain started radiating through my skull.

This one was different though.

I never had a migraine come on so fast before.

I was seven when the hallucinations first started, and migraines were never a part of it. But as the years progressed the headaches grew worse and worse. Now they were at a debilitating level. The pain was usually so unbearable that I'd have no choice but to curl up in a ball on the bathroom floor with tears streaming down my cheeks, just waiting for it to end.

Through the pain I'd see flashes of a person dying, but it wasn't just a typical death. I couldn't just see someone passing quietly in their sleep. Oh, no. I had to see people being murdered. People having their lives ripped away from them at the hands of another person as they fought to escape. I never saw the person doing the killing, just the victim, and as if *seeing* their fear wasn't enough, I had to *feel* it as well. Every thought that went through their minds, every emotion they experienced, the bone-chilling terror coursing through their veins as they died.

I rushed to the bathroom as fast as I could. Bright flashes of light from the pain in my head blurred my vision, to the point that I wasn't sure where I was going. I didn't quite make it to the toilet before the searing pain caused my stomach to expel its contents for the second time in one day.

Visions of a blonde woman were flashing behind my closed eyelids.

Something wasn't right though. Instead of being an outsider experiencing this girl's pain, I felt like I *was* her. That couldn't be right. She had blonde hair to my brown. From the flashes, I could tell that she was much taller than me. Things weren't adding up.

I heard her screaming.

I felt panicked as she ran from someone.

But I couldn't see her face. Why couldn't I see her face?

Her back stayed to me the whole time as bits and pieces of her death came at me with the force of a sledge hammer against concrete.

This isn't right.

That was the last thought I had before the pain grew to be too much and blackness consumed me.

The Poet

I was becoming discouraged. The last woman I thought was special turned out to be nothing more than a pathetic liar. I'd given her a chance to be my soul mate and she'd thrown it back in my face by claiming to be married. I followed her around long enough to know that wasn't true.

She'd disappointed me and for that, she had to suffer the consequences. The only thing my filthy whore of a mother had ever taught me was that women were never to be trusted.

But the romantic in me refused to believe it. I knew in my heart that there was a woman out there who was meant just for me. I just needed to find her.

I'd been coming to Cherry Street Coffee House for a few weeks for one reason. It wasn't the coffee; there was a better coffee house just a few blocks down the street.

No, it was the beautiful barista that stood behind the counter every morning. She'd called me handsome the first morning I walked in and hope sprang to life inside of me. After Sylvia, I wasn't sure I'd be able to find another love, but she graced me with that gorgeous smile and I was helpless.

"Good morning, lovely Samantha," I greeted, as I took my turn to order. The bright smile she normally shot at me most mornings seemed a little strained.

"Good morning, sir. What can I get you?"

Why was she speaking to me with such formality? I thought we'd moved passed that over the last few days.

I smiled wider in an attempt to pull her from whatever unpleasant thoughts were keeping her from paying me the attention I deserved. "I'm doing well. But I'll admit my day would be perfect if you would agree to join me for dinner." It was the second time I had extended the invitation and she'd do well to accept it.

She fidgeted behind the counter and averted her eyes. The fact that she wouldn't maintain eye contact angered me.

"I'm sorry but I'm in a relationship."

For weeks, I watched her from the shadows. I knew there wasn't a man in her life so why was she lying to me? Didn't she know what I was capable of giving her?

I felt the anger churning deep inside, threatening to take over.

She wasn't special after all.

She was just like the rest of them…a dirty, lying whore.

And she was going to have to pay for her sins.

Taylor

I am not yours, not lost in you,
Not lost, although I long to be
Lost as a candle lit at noon,
Lost as a snowflake in the sea.

You love me, and I find you still
A spirit beautiful and bright,
Yet I am I, who long to be
Lost as a light is lost in light.

Oh plunge me deep in love — put out
My senses, leave me deaf and blind,
Swept by the tempest of your love,
A taper is a rushing wind.

I can't move. I'm lying on what feels like a mattress, a hard coil poking me in the back. As I move around dust and God only knows what else billows from the mattress and clogs my nose. The smell is putrid and sour. My arms extend above my head like they're tied to something, but when I try and pull against the restraints there's nothing there. I'm bound and struggling, spread out on a disgusting mattress, fighting against air. I try to kick my legs but experience the same thing.

What's going on?

Where am I?

I turn my head from side to side, trying to make out anything that can tell me where I am, but all I see is black. There are no signs of light anywhere.

I may not know where I am, but I do know I'm not alone. I can sense someone in the room with me but I'm too frightened to call out...too afraid of who might answer.

Suddenly, something cold glides across my bare stomach and realization hits me. I'm naked. Whoever has me, has tied me down like an animal and stripped me of my clothes. The object on my skin slides over my ribs and across my breasts, the chill from it causing my nipples to harden. I can't hold back the sob that escapes my mouth knowing my body is being violated.

The object that slides up my neck to my cheek feels like metal, but I can't see well enough to be certain. My senses are fuzzy from whatever the person used to drug me. Without warning, the cold metal twists and burrows through the flesh on my cheek. Even with all the adrenaline coursing through me, I can feel the pain travel through every nerve ending in my body.

I let out a scream of pain and try to wrench my arms free while whoever is in the room hovers over me. It's a knife, a very sharp knife and whoever is holding it just cut me down to the bone.

I hear the sound of a man chuckling as I fight against my invisible bonds and a sudden, paralyzing fear courses through my body bringing my struggles to a sudden halt.

"Please," I beg as tears pour down my face. "Please, whoever you are...just let me go. I won't tell. I swear I won't. Just let me go." My voice breaks at the end and the person in the room with me laughs harder and pushes the blade of the knife against my stomach. I feel it break the skin and I start to thrash around again in an attempt to get away.

I'm going to die here; I can feel it in every bone in my body. I'm not leaving this room alive.

"Tell me you love me," he says once I've stopped struggling.

I know that voice. Oh God, I know this man, but I can't think of who he is. The pain from where he's cut me is so overwhelming I can't concentrate. Where have I heard that voice?

"Tell me you love me and I'll let you go," he says.

I want to believe him. I'm desperate to believe him, but something tells me it's not true. He won't let me go.

But I say it anyway. I have to at least try. "I love you," I cry out between sobs.

He leans closer and I can smell the soap on his skin. His scent is as familiar as his voice. "I don't believe you!" He hisses, pure rage and evil in his voice. That's the last thing I hear before the knife plunges in.

I shot up so fast my head bashed against the side of the toilet. Just like with every nightmare, I was covered in sweat and breathing erratically. Once I finally came to my senses and looked at my surroundings, I realized I was sitting on my bathroom floor.

I closed my eyes and fought against my foggy brain; desperately trying to remember what had happened. It all came back to me in slow motion. The migraine, the violent vomiting, the pain, the flashes of blonde hair. I must have blacked out on my bathroom floor.

Once I was stable enough, I pulled myself off the floor and reached over to turn on the shower. The only thing I could think of doing was to wash the horrible images in my mind away. I stripped off the uniform I was still wearing from work and climbed under the scalding spray, hoping the hot water would do the trick.

I reached for the shower poof and poured a generous amount of body wash onto it. As I scrubbed my skin pieces of my dream started to come back to me. I lightly ran my finger across my cheek, feeling nothing but the water rolling down my face. Then I inspected my stomach. There was nothing there. No cuts, no blood, not even a red mark.

But it all felt so real. Every time that knife cut the woman in my dream I could swear I felt it.

Enough was enough. I was calling Dr. Kinsley first thing in the morning. I didn't know how much longer I could last, going at the rate I was.

I quickly finished up in the shower, cut the water and stepped out. I dried off and didn't even bother to run a brush through my hair. I threw on the first t-shirt I touched, stepped into my underwear and collapsed into bed. All of my fears of falling asleep were pushed away. The hallucinations and nightmare had drained everything out of me and by the time my head hit the pillow, I was out.

When I woke the next morning, the first thing I did was call Dr. Kinsley's office to book the first available appointment, but as soon as the receptionist informed me she couldn't get me in for another two weeks, I slammed the phone down in defeat.

I didn't think I had two weeks in me. I felt like I was losing my mind and with each passing day that feeling got worse and worse.

I did the only thing I could do and started getting ready for work. I pulled my red Benny's Diner shirt over my head and stepped into a pair of black shorts. It was an unusually sunny day by Seattle's standards, but I just couldn't find it in me to appreciate the beauty of it.

My hair was a disaster from sleeping on it wet and not brushing it out, so the only option I had was to throw it up in a messy bun on the crown of my head. I tossed my nametag and cell phone into my purse and head out the door.

I kept replaying the flashes from the nightmare over and over again, letting my feet guide me along the familiar route to the diner. I knew it like the back of my hand. I was capable of walking it without even paying attention, which wasn't normally a big deal.

Until today.

I looked up, straight into a pair of mesmerizing crystal blue eyes.

Son of a bitch!

Almost as if he'd read my thoughts, a smile stretched across his face. "The paper you read last night warned you to be sure to take in your surroundings."

In any other circumstance, I might have been scared to see him there—don't misunderstand me, seeing him did make me a little nervous—but I was on a crowded sidewalk in downtown Seattle. It wasn't like he could snatch me up without anyone noticing.

I narrowed my eyes at him as he took a step closer. "All right, asshole..." That caused him to stop moving. "I don't know what kind of sick fuck you are or how the hell you know all these things about me but it's obvious you're some sort of degenerate stalker. You need to stay the hell away from me or I swear to God, I'll scream rape at the top of my lungs."

He shook his head and the expression was one akin to how a parent would look at a disobedient child. "First of all, I'm not a degenerate stalker and second...seriously? Who screams rape on a crowded sidewalk? What are you, twelve? I'm not even touching you."

The sarcasm in his tone set me off. All my nervousness disappeared and the only thing I wanted to do was kick his ass. He let out a snort and looked me up and down. "Not likely to happen shorty, but you're welcome to try."

What. The...

"Fuck," he finished out loud. "Yeah, yeah, we get it. You've got a potty mouth. You should be so proud." I felt my mouth drop open and my eyes bug out. I was struck utterly speechless. "We need to talk," he continued once he realized I wasn't going to respond.

"What the...how did you...Holy shit! It happened. It finally fucking happened!" I said with a laugh that probably came out sounding a little demented. "I've gone *completely* crazy. The last shred of sanity I had just got blown the hell up. You're probably not even real are you? Wait...why am I asking you? You're not real, just a figment of my insane imagination." Daniel let out a sigh, rolled his eyes and leaned against the

brick wall like he already knew I wasn't even close to being
finished.

"That's another sign of insanity, isn't it? Talking to my
apparition…or talking to myself for that matter. Oh my God,
I'm doing it right now. *Son of a bitch*!" I continued on with my
rant. I was sure I was scaring the people around me. Hell, I was
starting to scare myself.

"Is there any chance you could wrap this drama up ASAFP
so we can get to the important shit, please? I'm kind of here
for a reason."

"ASAFP?" I asked, ignoring everything else he'd just said.

"Yeah, as in as soon as fucking possible."

"Who's the potty mouth now?"

Yep, I'm certifiable.

Daniel grabbed hold of both my shoulders and gave me a
slight shake before doing that double finger eye point thingy
back and forth between us. "Concentrate please." I tried to
pull myself together as best as I could. "You aren't going crazy,
I'm not an apparition, and if you'd just shut up, I'd be more
than happy to explain what's going on."

My back went straight at the seriousness in his tone and I
felt a prickle of alarm. Instinct told me not to dismiss
him…that what he had to say was real. He was real and I
needed to listen to him. "But you said yesterday I wasn't ready.
And guess what? I'm still not ready."

He let go of my shoulders and ran both hands through his
inky black hair in frustration. "Yeah, well that vision you had
last night kind of bumped things up. Shit's accelerating and I'm
running out of time."

I shook my head, trying to make sense of what he was
saying. "Wait…accelerating? What's accelerating? And running
out of time for what?"

He grabbed my hand and started pulling me in the
direction I was originally heading in. "Come on. I'll explain
over coffee."

"How did you…oh, hell, never mind."

I heard him chuckle as he pulled me along the sidewalk and through the door of the coffee shop I frequented. "She's finally catching on. It's a miracle."

"He's still a smartass. What a shocker," I replied.

He dragged me to a booth near the back window that was a little more private and deposited me in my seat. "You know, most women would be falling over themselves for my attention. I'm kind of a panty melter," he said as he waved his hands in front of his torso.

"You didn't just say that," I replied with a roll of my eyes.

His lips kicked up on one side as he leaned in and lowered his voice. It was obvious he was shooting for seductive, but I was immune. "You can't honestly say you haven't noticed how good looking I am. I know for a fact you have."

I crossed my arms on the table and smiled. "Then you opened your mouth and all that pretty went to shit."

He threw his head back and let out a gut busting laugh. It took him a second, but once he finally got himself together he pretended to wipe a tear from his eye, patted me on the head and informed me, "Be right back, shorty," before heading up to the counter to get our drinks.

By the time he got back with our coffees the good humor had vanished from his face and everything about his body language screamed it was time to get serious.

"I'm not exactly sure how to dump this all on you so I'm just going to start from the beginning. I need you to try your best to keep an open mind and let me finish before you say anything. You think you can do that?"

All I could do was nod my head in response as I reached for my grandmother's locket around my neck.

He inhaled deeply, held it for a few seconds, and then blew it out. "First of all, let me explain what happened yesterday. When we shook hands you caught glimpses of the past, but something was different about them, right?"

Again, I nodded.

"Those were my memories, Taylor. I've been with you since your seventh birthday."

I wasn't sure I understood. "You mean, like we grew up together or something?"

He ran a hand over his face before lifting his coffee cup and taking a long drink. I followed suit. "No, we didn't grow up together. This would be the part where you need to keep an open mind."

"Okaaaay." I dragged the word out; suddenly nervous about what was coming next.

"I'm what is referred to as a Guide. I'm assigned to a Seer and it's my job to make sure that person stays on track and does the job they're supposed to do. You're a Seer, Taylor. I was assigned to you when you turned seven and I've been with you ever since. That's why I knew your birth name was Lydia Taylor and you had it legally changed to Taylor Carmichael when you turned eighteen. That's why you felt a connection with me in the diner yesterday. Subconsciously, you know I've always been there, you just weren't fully aware of it until now."

"What's—"

He interrupted before I could finish. "A Seer?" he asked.

"Yes. What does that even mean?"

He placed his arms on the table and clasped his hands in front of him. "A Seer is a person gifted with the ability to see death before it happens."

A gasp rushed past my lips as my eyes grew wide. "My hallucinations?"

"Stop calling them that, Taylor. They're visions. Visions that you've been ignoring since you were a child."

He seemed almost disappointed when he said that.

I reached for the locket again and began rubbing my thumb in a circle over the smooth surface.

When I looked up, I caught Daniel watching my hand with a knowing expression and a question popped into my head.

Did you know my grandmother?

I hadn't spoken out loud, but Daniel still responded.

He gave me a sad smile and shook his head. "No, I wasn't her Guide. But despite what you were raised to believe, she wasn't crazy and neither are you."

I felt tears sting the back of my eyes and I blinked rapidly in an attempt to stop them. "How do you do that? And how the hell do you know what I'm thinking before I say it?"

"It's all a part of the job as your Guide. I'm able to access your thoughts when I feel it's necessary."

I let out a snort at his response. "And I guess I'm just supposed to trust that you don't abuse that nifty little power?"

There was that smile again. "I never said that."

I felt a heat creeping up and dropped my eyes to where my hands were fisted in my lap. "You have to know that this all sounds completely ridiculous. I mean, this is shit out of the movies, not real life, Daniel. Why should I even believe what you're saying?"

He nodded and I could feel his eyes boring into me. I lifted my head and was instantly sucked in. It was as if he was in control and wouldn't let my gaze waver off of his. "I can understand that it's a lot to take in but there's something inside you that knows what I'm saying is the truth, even if you don't want to believe it." He was right. I couldn't explain why, but deep in my gut I knew everything he was saying was true. "And this isn't a movie," he continued. "This is serious shit. You've been given a gift and you're wasting it."

The red in my face was no longer from blushing; it was pure anger. "How dare you," I hissed between clenched teeth. "Who the fuck says this is a gift? It's not a gift, it's a goddamn curse!" I yelled.

Daniel glanced around quickly to make sure no one overheard. "Keep your voice down, Taylor," he scolded.

"Fuck you!" I shouted back, catching the unwanted attention of several customers.

I worked on taking deep cleansing breaths before I reached across the table and ripped Daniel's head off. "If you've been with me since I was seven then you *know*. You *know* the absolute hell that my life has been. You know how scared I was when all this started. The shit my parents put me through because they thought I was nuts just like my grandmother. The psychiatrists, the torment from my classmates..." Daniel visibly flinched as I ticked off the list of horrible events in my life that proved my visions were, in fact, a majorly fucked up curse. "Where were you through all of that, huh? If you were supposed to help me, where were you?" My last words broke as tears clogged my throat.

It was his turn to look down at his hands. "It's not the job of a Guide to protect the Seer," he whispered.

My head snapped back like I'd been slapped. "Fuck you, Daniel."

His head shot up and he narrowed his eyes at me. "You don't think I would have helped you if I could have? You don't think I would have given anything to make your life a little better?"

I slapped my hands on the table and leaned closer to him. "No, I don't!" I shouted.

"Well you're wrong!" he yelled back. We were back to gathering unwanted attention again. "It killed me having to watch you go through all of that, but I couldn't do anything. The consequences would have been unbearable for the both of us if I'd intervened. My hands were tied, Taylor."

"Then what changed?" I demanded. "Why are you allowed to step up now but not back when I was just a little kid, scared to death of the things I was seeing? Why not when I really needed you?"

"Because this is it, Taylor!"

I immediately recoiled. Not at his yelling but at his words. We both remained silent for a long time while Daniel tried to calm himself and I tried to process what he just said. Finally, I whispered, "This is it? What does that mean?"

He put his elbows on the table heavily and I cringed at the pain that must have caused. He placed his head in his palms and scrubbed his face. "Whether you believe in God, Allah, Buddha or whoever you choose to worship, the fact is, there is a higher power out there. When that higher power created humanity, the theory of natural selection was put into play but lines began to be crossed so often that they eventually blurred. The evil that wasn't taken into consideration started causing the numbers to become…uneven. The Seers were created to level the metaphorical playing field, so to speak. The people that come to you in those visions are innocents who aren't meant to die yet. Evil has intervened and plans to take them before their time and it's up to the Seer to try and prevent that death before it happens."

I felt like my head might explode from everything he was saying. It was too much to take in.

"There can only be so many Seers and when one isn't doing their job of saving the lives that are taken before their time then…eventually, their visions start to fade. That's what's happening to you right now. You've ignored your visions for so long you weren't able to see the woman's face in the vision you had last night. There comes a point where you can't get that back and you're almost at that point, Taylor."

I took a second to process his words and decided that it didn't seem like a bad thing. I'd wanted the visions to stop from the moment they began. "I'm okay with that. I don't want these visions. I don't want this fucking gift. Let them take it back."

He shook his head and I knew I wasn't going to like what he was about to say. "It doesn't work that way. Your visions will never fully disappear but you won't be any good as a Seer because you can't *see* who it is you're supposed to be helping. I already told you there can only be so many of your kind. If you don't start embracing your visions and do what you can to help the people you see, then another Seer must be born to take your place."

"Okay. So let another one be born. I'll gladly step aside for them to take over."

He let out a frustrated growl. "Taylor, listen to me carefully. For another Seer to be born with their full gift, one must die to relinquish all of the power that they hold." He paused to see if his words were sinking in then drove his point home. "If you don't start doing the job that was given to you, you won't make it to your twenty-fourth birthday."

Everything stopped; the noise from the people around us, the grinding of the espresso maker, the clanging sounds of the baristas working behind the counter. Everything was silent except for the blood rushing in my ears. I hadn't realized I was holding my breath until the pressure in my chest brought me back to reality. I sucked in a breath and pinned Daniel with a hard stare. "So you're saying my only options are to live the rest of my life seeing things that will more than likely drive me insane or die? All because I'm being punished for not using a gift I didn't want in the first fucking place!"

"I'm sorry," he stated weakly.

"You're sorry. I'm going to die or go crazy and all I get from you is 'I'm sorry'? Wow, you really suck at this. How in the hell did you even get this job anyway? Because I seriously think you need a demotion or something."

"I had just as much choice in it as you did," he demanded somewhat coldly. My insults had obviously hit their mark.

A bitter laugh bubbled up in my throat and I couldn't hold it back. "Then what a pair we make, huh? Just two people being royally screwed by the universe."

When the tears I'd been holding back finally broke free Daniel reached for my hands and laced our fingers together on top of the table. "I'm doing everything I can, Taylor. Now that I'm actually allowed to intervene I've been doing everything in my power to get through to you."

"The nightmares," I guessed.

He gave a slight nod and looked almost heartbroken. "It was the only way. The dreams were the only way I could keep these women at the forefront of your mind. Once you accept this and start trying to help, your visions will come back to their full strength and the dreams will stop."

I pulled my hands from his and reached for my purse. "Nightmares, Daniel, not dreams. There's a huge difference. What you've been doing has resulted in a total of eight hours of sleep in a week. I'm terrified to close my eyes at night."

I stood up and started to step away from the table when his voice followed after me. "Embrace this, Taylor. Please. I can't save you if you don't and I've already failed you enough as it is."

I turned back and looked at his face. He really was handsome even when his eyes were squeezed shut and his forehead was creased in defeat. "Your hands were tied just as much as mine were." Daniel's eyes popped open and narrowed on me as I spoke. "You've done your job so you can sleep easy now. At least you have that. I've got to get to work."

And with that, I turned, walked out the door of the coffee shop and left Daniel to stare after me.

When I pushed through the door of Benny's, I was twenty minutes late for my shift. Cassie came rushing up to me with worry etched on her pretty face. "Taylor, are you okay? You look upset."

I tried to smile, but my lips didn't want to cooperate. "I'm fine, just slept through my alarm. Is Benny mad?"

I heard her approach me from behind. "Of course I'm not mad," Benny replied in a raspy voice. "Child, you haven't been late for a shift in the five years you've been here. I wasn't mad, I was worried."

"Thank you for the concern but everything's fine." I tried to walk around her and toward the back office to drop my purse, but for an older, out of shape woman, Benny was surprisingly quick on her feet. She cut me off before I could even take one step. "You haven't been sleeping, you're late for work, and I didn't want to bring it up, but...well...you've lost quite a bit of weight, sweetheart."

I placed my hands on my waist and leveled her with a stare. I had the utmost respect for my boss, but that didn't mean she couldn't piss me off. "What are you trying to say, Benny?"

I shouldn't have asked.

"I'm saying you look like shit and you need a vacation," she responded with the attitude I could imagine a mother using on her teenage daughter.

My mouth dropped open as Cassie stood beside me laughing hysterically.

"Unbelievable," I grumbled as I pushed past her and stalked to the office. "I'm not taking a vacation so deal with it," I called over my shoulder.

"Well if you keel over in the middle of the dinner rush, don't expect me to do more than step over your boney little body. It'll be your own damn fault."

This day can't possibly get any worse.

I threw my purse into my locker with a little too much force and the contents spilled out, rolling all over the floor.

I spoke too soon.

I was more pissed off than I'd ever been as I snatched up an apron, leaving my purse and everything in it on the floor, and headed out to the dining room. I was starting to look forward to losing myself in the monotony of my day when I heard a voice that had my eyes rolling in annoyance.

"Well, well, well. Looky what we have here. You're looking mighty fine this morning if I do say so myself," Stevens, formerly known as Stank Breath called out.

I'd never been one for confrontation. I'd spent my life shying away from anything that could draw attention to myself, but his pompous attitude had me wanting to yell out something that could have possibly gotten me fired. That was, until I spun around and saw that he was sitting with Jordan. If he looked good yesterday, he was damn near edible today.

He'd looked fine in jeans and a Henley when I'd first seen him, but today he was in a white button down shirt with the cuffs folded up to his elbows, showing off his thick, muscular forearms. My blood heated and I felt like butterflies were going crazy deep in my belly. Seeing as I'd never allowed myself to get too close to people before, my instant reaction to him confused the hell out of me. I wanted to get closer…wanted to explore all of the new feelings he brought out in me and that was a very dangerous feeling.

It didn't make sense, especially considering I knew nothing about him, but the turmoil that was constantly floating around me seemed to lessen whenever he was around. I didn't know if I should be concerned with the fact that a man I hadn't even known for twenty-four hours could affect me the way he was, but I couldn't stop the heady rush I felt from wanting him that swept over me just by looking at him.

He made me feel things I didn't know how to describe. I'd never felt more alive, but at the same time, scared out of my mind. It felt exhilarating just being near him. I'd never experienced anything like it in my twenty-three years and a large part of me hoped that I'd feel that way for years to come.

Then sadness dragged me down faster than I ever thought possible. My earlier conversation with Daniel let me know I might not have many years left to live. I might not have the chance to know what it felt like to have a boyfriend or to love someone else. I might not ever get the chance to really lose myself in a man. I was being dragged down by the decision I had to make, lost to the sadness it caused. That high I was feeling just moments before was gone.

As if he sensed the change in my demeanor, the smile slipped from his sexy lips and a frown creased his brow. "What can I get you guys?" I asked, not taking my eyes off my pad.

"Reuben for me and turkey club for this asshole here," Stevens replied.

I scribbled down their order, and then before I could stop myself, my mouth opened and the words just poured out. I never initiated conversations with other people but I found myself wanting to do or say something just so I could hear Jordan's voice. "Same sandwiches two days in a row. Either the food here is better than I thought or you guys can't cook for shit."

Stevens let out a loud guffaw and slapped the table. "Nah, the food's okay but not that good. We just came back 'cause this loser's got a thing for ya and was in the mood to get shot down a second time. He offered to pay so I thought why the hell not?"

My head shot up in surprise and I flicked my gaze from Stevens to Jordan who looked about ready to commit murder. "You're paying for your own damn meal now, dickhead."

Stevens let out a groan that caused his potbelly to jiggle and I feared for the buttons on his shirt. "Ah, come on man. I was just laying the foundation for you."

"Go sit over there," Jordan said with a growl as he pointed to another table.

Stevens grumbled under his breath as he stood and made his way to the other table *not* in my section. I couldn't make out everything he said, but I was pretty sure I heard douche bag, cock sucker, and—my favorite of them all—son of a horse faced crack head. I had to hand it to Stevens, he was a tool, but at least he was a colorful one.

I tried to suppress my laughter as I turned back to Jordan, but when I caught him biting on his bottom lip to keep from laughing himself, I couldn't hold it in any longer. After a second, Jordan joined in and the sound of his laughter warmed my soul. Thoughts of pressing my lips to that beautiful mouth flooded my brain.

"Sorry about him," he grumbled once we'd pulled ourselves together.

"No problem. We already established yesterday that he had some permanent brain damage."

He rubbed the back of his neck in nervous strokes. "It seems like every conversation we have starts with me apologizing. Maybe I'll get it right one day."

I bent my head to try and obstruct his view of my reddening cheeks, but I knew it didn't work. At that moment I would have given anything for a tan just to hide the flush on my face. "There it is," he murmured and I could hear the smile in his voice. "Ahhh…there's the blush." His eyes warmed. "You're beautiful, Crimson."

I looked at him with a small smile. "Thank you," I whispered so low I knew it was barely audible.

I fumbled with my pad and pen and tried to beat a hasty retreat. "I'll just go put in your order."

Before I could walk away, he spoke. "He might be a jackass but he's right, you know."

"I'm sorry?"

"Stevens. He's right. I came back hoping for another shot. I'm more prepared this time though. I gave myself a pep talk in front of the mirror this morning and everything."

The cheeky grin he gave me showcased his perfect teeth and lips and I was surprised to see that he had dimples.

His lightheartedness was quickly rubbing off on me, because before I knew it, I was playing right into his trap and flirting back. "A pep talk, huh? How'd that work for you?"

"Pretty good actually. Myself told me that I'm a reasonably attractive, thirty-something with a 401K and dental insurance. We're fairly positive that I'm a total catch, and we both think you'd have a great time if you let me take you out."

I cocked my hip and crossed my arms over my chest. "You know you sound a little certifiable right now, don't you?" I asked through a grin.

"Myself says it's all part of my charm."

I caught movement out of the corner of my eye and glanced over to see Benny and Cassie huddled together at the hostess stand. Their undivided attention was on mine and Jordan's interaction and there was no masking huge grins on each of their faces.

I shook my head at my friends and turned my attention back to Jordan. "Yourself might be lying to you," I teased, surprised that I was actually flirting *again*.

"What if I told you I also had medical insurance and own my own home that my mother *does not* live in?"

For the second time in as many days, I laughed a real, genuine laugh deep from within. "When you put it that way, how could a girl resist?"

He clapped his hands together in triumph. "I knew I'd wear you down. Now give me your number before you have time to change your mind."

I quickly scrawled my number on a blank order slip and passed it his way. He pulled out his wallet and slid it in carefully like he was taking extra care not to wrinkle it.

I'd just taken a major leap into the unknown, and while it was scary, it was a completely different, exciting kind of fear.

Jordan

"You've seen the girl two times for all of five minutes. How is it that you're already pussy whipped?" Stevens asked.

I swear to Christ…if Barry Stevens wasn't my partner, I'd murder him. I was seriously contemplating it as it was. He'd been on my ass all day long about what went down at the diner that morning.

"I'm not pussy whipped, you moron. It's called courting. You should try it some time. Maybe if you'd do more than grunt and leer at women like a pervert you'd actually get someone else to play with your dick for once."

"My dick gets played with plenty, fuck you very much."

I let out a derisive laugh as I got in the driver side of the car while Stevens squeezed his gut into the passenger seat. He was wrong. I wasn't pussy whipped, but there was definitely something about Taylor that enthralled me…and it wasn't just that she was beautiful. But Christ, that girl was beautiful. Long, dark, wavy hair that went almost all the way to that perfect ass of hers made me want to wrap it around my fist as I took her. The woman had curves that would tempt a priest. But it was her eyes that drew me in the most. They were the most unique brown I'd ever seen, almost like burnished copper. Despite how gorgeous they were, there was a sadness behind them that shouldn't have been there. Her eyes held so much sorrow and I felt compelled to make it better.

There was no doubt in my mind that she was several years younger than I was and had obviously experienced something bad in her life that made her hesitant. The nervousness that radiated off of her was almost palpable and I usually ran in the other direction when it came to women with that much drama, but I couldn't stay away from her. I hardly knew her, yet I was already certain that if she gave me the chance, I'd do everything in my power to take that pain away. It didn't make sense. I wanted to know her. I *needed* to know her. And in just a few more hours I was going to get my chance.

I'd been on countless dates in my life, but for the first time ever, I was actually anxious at the thought of taking the beautiful Taylor out.

Huh…maybe I *was* pussy whipped.

If I was anxious I could only imagine how Taylor was fairing considering nervous seemed to be the norm for her. She was probably freaking the hell out. I started to wonder if she was considering bailing on the date and decided I should cut her off at the pass, just in case. I pulled out my cell and scrolled down to her number.

Tonight was happening no matter what.

Taylor

Oh God, what the hell was I thinking saying yes to Jordan? I'd never been on a date before, yet I picked Jordan as my foray into the dating world; a good looking man who was probably an expert at all things relating to women. Instead of dipping my toe in the kiddy pool I'd just cannon balled right into the deep end.

Shit.

Even yoga wasn't helping. I was currently in my living room, spread out on the floor in child's pose. I should have been relaxed…centered, but instead I was hyperventilating and about two seconds away from a full blown panic attack.

That's it, I'm cancelling.

I didn't care if Cassie threatened to kick my ass before I left work earlier. I couldn't go through with it. Agreeing to a date with Jordan was a mistake. After all, it wasn't as if I didn't have more important, essentially life ending decisions I needed to concentrate on. I should have been worrying about that rather than freaking out over a stupid date that wouldn't even matter in the long run. Nothing was going to be able to come from the date anyway. I was destined to end up either crazy or dead. Nowhere in either of those scenarios was room for a relationship.

I was right in the middle of thinking up a good excuse when my cell phone chimed.

> *J: If I was a betting man I'd lay down money that you're having second thoughts.*

How could he have possibly known that? Was he another Daniel or something? God, I really hoped that wasn't the case.

> *T: What makes you say that?*

> *J: You seem nervous by nature so I was just guessing.*

He wasn't another Daniel...just an intuitive know it all. My phone chimed again a few seconds later.

> *J: So am I right??*

I wasn't willing to admit to him that he was. He already seemed cocky enough so I did the one thing that always came naturally...I lied.

> *T: Well, I wasn't but I am now. Not cuz I'm nervous, but cuz you seem like a jackass.*

He texted back almost instantly.

> *J: LOL. Not a jackass, just anxious to see you. Don't cancel...Please.*

I felt ridiculous. I was sitting on my living room floor by myself blushing like an idiot because of a single text message.

> *I'm in trouble.*

I dug in my closet for the better part of an hour trying to find something that qualified as "nice". My wardrobe mainly consisted of work uniforms, jeans, yoga pants, t-shirts and Chuck Taylors. After what seemed like forever, I finally managed to locate my one and only dress; a navy wrap dress that Benny bought me for my last birthday.

It had a neckline that dipped a little low but not enough to make me look slutty. It fell a few inches above my knees and hugged my curves in a very flattering way. When I'd unwrapped the box it had come in, the first thing I'd thought was that I was never going to have the opportunity to wear it.

At that very moment I could have kissed her for buying it for me. I blew my hair dry and added just enough product to keep my waves under control. Makeup was never my thing so I kept it simple with a small amount of blush, a touch of eye shadow, mascara and nude gloss.

I paired the dress with the only pair of shoes I had that weren't Chucks or flip flops; a pair of tan sling back, peep-toe heels that also—not surprisingly—came from Benny. I'd been pacing the length of my apartment for the past ten minutes and nearly jumped out of my skin when I heard a knock on the door. Other than the pizza or Chinese takeout delivery guys no one really ever knocked on my door.

I opened the door and my breath caught in my lungs. The man standing in front of me was utter perfection. His black dress slacks hugged his muscular thighs in a way that should have been illegal. He wore a dove gray button down with the top two buttons undone under a black suit jacket. Visions of me licking the small amount of skin peeking out from his collar swam through my head, causing a full body shiver.

I was pulled out of my daze when he finally spoke. "Wow. Taylor, you look amazing."

I ducked my head and fiddled with the locket around my neck. "Uh…thanks," I said in a quiet voice. "You look really nice too."

He placed a finger under my chin and lifted my face so that I met those hazel eyes head on. "Do you have any clue how sexy you are when you blush?"

My eyes grew wide and my lips parted to respond, but I couldn't form words. I'd never had a man call me sexy before, especially a man that was the walking, breathing definition of the word itself. "Please don't hide it from me."

I swallowed hard, gave a small nod and whispered, "Okay."

A smirk spread across his lips before he said, "I kind of like that I have that affect on you because the feeling's mutual."

I'd never done it before, but I was pretty sure I just swooned. "I affect you?" I asked, surprised.

"Crimson, you have no idea."

He reached up and tucked a lock of hair behind my ear before trailing his fingers across my shoulder. His fingers whispered down my arm to my hand where he laced them together and gave it a little tug. "You ready to go?"

"Yeah, just give me a second." I pulled the door open a little further for him to step in as I went to grab my clutch.

"This apartment's amazing," he pointed out, as he took in the surroundings.

It really was.

If my parents were going to insist on paying for me to stay out of their lives then I figured I might as well live nicely. Granite countertops and dark, hardwood spread throughout the space. It wasn't a huge apartment so I had it furnished with the most comfortable, plush furniture I could find. But I didn't want to get into all the reasons why a waitress at a diner would live in such an expensive place so I just said, "family money," and left it at that, hoping he'd catch on as I guided him out the door and locked it behind me.

He took my hand again as he led me to the elevator and I was surprised to find that the contact didn't bother me in the slightest. It didn't feel like I'd just met Jordan the day before. I felt a sense of comfort when I was around him. He was the only person I'd ever met that could make me feel safe. As we waited for the elevator, I decided to try and dig for information again. "So are you finally going to let me in on where we're going?"

I saw him smile and shake his head out of the corner of my eye. "You really don't like surprises, do you?" he asked with a laugh.

I smiled and shook my head, "Not really."

"You like steak?"

The safety I always felt in his presence was beginning to have a calming effect and I was actually able to relax. "If it's cooked right."

"Well then you're in luck," he responded as he led me into the waiting elevator. "Canlis makes the best filet mignon you'll ever have."

"That's where we're going?" I'd never been there, but I knew it wasn't cheap and it was pretty difficult to get a table at the last minute.

We exited the elevator and he placed his hand at the small of my back to direct me through the lobby. "Luckily, I was able to get a reservation. It took some fancy talk on my part so feel free to be impressed."

I laughed and glanced over to see Gary sitting behind his desk, smiling warmly at me from over the top of his latest Stephen King novel. "Enjoy your night, Taylor," he called as we walked past. The look on his face was similar to what I could only guess a proud father would look like.

"Thanks, Gary, you too. I've got some muffins already baked for you in the morning."

He placed a hand over his heart. "You're too good to me, sweetheart."

Jordan and I walked out the doors into the mild Seattle night to a black Toyota Sequoia. He disengaged the locks and opened the passenger door to help me in before heading around the front of the car, getting in on the driver side.

"Should I be jealous?" he asked with humor laced through his words.

"Of Gary?"

He smiled, showing off his dimples and nodded.

"Well, I guess you could be. But seeing as he's madly in love with his wife of thirty-two years you might be wasting your time. Besides, he's like a father to me." The affection was evident in my voice whenever I talked about Gary...or Benny. They were like the parents I never had.

"Where's your dad?" he asked as he merged into traffic and started for the restaurant. I knew there would be questions about my family and childhood, but I didn't think I'd ever be properly prepared to discuss my past.

"My parents are in Connecticut. I moved out here when I graduated." I left it at that hoping he wouldn't ask anymore about them, but I wasn't so lucky.

"Did you move out here for college or something?"

I looked out the window as the city passed by in a blur. "No, I didn't go to college. I just wanted to get away."

"And they were okay with you moving across the country by yourself?"

I directed my gaze to Jordan and he glanced away from the road to look at me. "I'm not really close with my family." I hoped my tone carried the message that my parents weren't really a topic I wanted to discuss. Thankfully, he seemed to understand.

We made idle conversation for the remainder of the drive and by the time we pulled up to the valet in front of the restaurant the mood in the car had lightened once again.

The valet opened my door and I stepped out as Jordan came around the car and joined me. "Ready?" he asked with that dimpled smile that I was really starting to love.

"Mm hmm."

He took my hand and led me into the restaurant.

That's when it hit me. I'd been so consumed with Jordan that I'd completely forgotten the fact that I didn't do well in crowded places. I was hit with a reminder the minute he pulled the door open and we stepped into the crowded restaurant. My chest tightened and my nerves came back full force.

I didn't know if I would be able to pull this off.

A bead of perspiration traveled from the nape of my neck, down my back.

"You okay?" Jordan whispered in my ear as we made our way to the hostess. At that moment I wished he wasn't so in tune with every slight shift in my mood. He'd had the ability to read me like a book from the first moment we'd laid eyes on each other.

All I could do was smile weakly and nod.

The slight frown across his brow told me he didn't believe me, but didn't push the matter and I appreciated it. "Reservation for Donovan," he said with a charming grin to the hostess and the pretty redhead lit up at Jordan's attention. Apparently, I wasn't the only one that he had an effect on. That was confirmed when I looked around the crowded area and saw every woman there giving Jordan an appreciative smile. At their obvious attention toward Jordan, I quickly realized that I was way out of my league.

Not only were the women paying attention to Jordan, they were sizing me up as well, causing my throat to dry up like the Sahara. I tried to swallow past the discomfort but it was useless.

I wasn't going to make it through dinner.

"Right this way," the redheaded hostess said with a seductive smile aimed right at Jordan. If I hadn't been minutes away from a panic attack, I might have found it in me to be pissed off at her blatant attempts to lure my date's attention to herself. But I had other things to worry about and I shot up a quick prayer that I wouldn't be hit with any visions during our meal.

We arrived at our table and Jordan pulled out my chair like a complete gentleman. I took my seat and kept my head down trying my best to avoid looking at anyone.

Our waiter came by and introduced himself before taking our drink order, but I made sure to barely glance in his direction. Jordan ordered a bottle of red wine and the waiter thankfully shuffled away quickly to go get it. "You sure you're okay, Taylor? You got really pale as soon as we walked through the door."

I tried to pull myself together and took a few deep, cleansing breaths. "I'm fine. I guess I didn't realize it would be so crowded."

Concern spread across his features and he reached across the table for my hand and began running his thumb over the back of it in soothing circles. "You have a problem with crowds?"

I ducked my head again and tried to hide my embarrassment behind the curtain of my hair. "Yeah, just a little," I replied as I reached for my locket again.

"Hey, can you look at me?" he asked as he tugged on my hand. I lifted my head slightly and gazed at him through my lashes. He looked so apologetic that I felt a pang of guilt at the thought of ruining our evening. "I'm so sorry, Taylor. If I'd known you had a problem with crowds I wouldn't have brought you here."

I felt defeated at his admission. Of course he wouldn't have bothered with me if he'd known what a freak I was. The last thing I wanted was for him to regret asking me out, so I did my best to suck it up and pasted a smile on my face.

"It's not a problem. I really am okay, I promise."

He smiled in return and the waiter came back with our bottle of wine. He poured us both a glass and I took a generous gulp, hoping it would fortify my nerves. We placed our order and all I could do was hope that service was speedy and we'd be out of here before I had the opportunity to embarrass myself any further. I pushed the noise of the busy restaurant out of my head and concentrated on the sexy-as-sin man in front of me. "So…Jordan Donovan, I know that you don't live with your mother, you have medical and dental insurance, you like to have conversations with yourself and you have a 401K. Anything else you feel like sharing about yourself?"

"Well, what would you like to know, Taylor…"

"Carmichael," I offered. "Taylor Carmichael."

"Beautiful name for a beautiful girl."

The blush returned but I didn't hide it from him this time. A genuine smile spread across his gorgeous lips and I knew he had noticed and that he appreciated it.

"Why don't we start with something simple? What do you do to earn that 401K?"

He let out a chuckle and took a sip of wine before answering. I copied and took another large gulp. I didn't intend to get drunk but I needed all the help I could get to make it through the evening. "I'm with the Seattle police department."

That surprised me. "You're a cop?"

He nodded, "Detective actually."

"Wow. Exactly how old are you, Detective Jordan Donovan?"

He looked a little hesitant before responding by telling me, "I don't know if I want to tell you that."

I tilted my head to the side, curious as to why he didn't want to answer my question. "Why not?"

He stared down at his butter knife like it was the most interesting thing he'd ever seen. "Because I have a feeling I'm a little older than you."

I let out a laugh at his admission. "That's all right. I'm twenty-three so I don't really mind you being a few years older. How old are you, twenty-seven? Twenty-eight? That's not a very big difference in my opinion."

He started twirling his wine glass by the stem, looking anywhere but at me. "Thirty-four," he finally mumbled causing my jaw to drop. I never would have guessed he was eleven years older than me. He looked so much younger. He finally looked up, taking in my open mouth. "Is that going to be a problem?"

Of course it wasn't a problem. I didn't have an issue with the age difference, I was just surprised. Jordan made me feel safe. Made me feel things I'd never felt before. It wouldn't have mattered if he was forty, I would have been an idiot to let a difference in age dictate how I felt about him when he was the only man who had ever been able to get past my defenses.

I closed my mouth and a smile easily spread across my face. He was kind of adorable when he was nervous. "Absolutely not." I responded and he graced me with that dimpled smile.

He blew out a relieved breath and grabbed my hand again, setting off a spark with his touch. "Thank Christ, because I have to tell you, I don't know if I'd have been able to let you go even if you couldn't deal with it. I know it sounds like a total cliché, but there's something about you. I need to know you. And I swear I'm not just saying that to get laid."

Warmth pooled in my belly at his words. "I feel the same," I admitted shyly.

Our waiter chose to return with our dinner right then, pulling us out of the moment and bursting the private little bubble we had been in. The sounds of the restaurant came back full force and I glanced around, taking in all the people surrounding me. There wasn't an empty table in sight. The wait staff bustled about, diners talked and laughed. It was the perfect setting to be bombarded with visions and it was absolutely stifling.

"Enjoy your meal," the waiter said before going to check on another table.

The air started to feel thicker with every passing second and my vision was becoming blurry. Dark shadows began creeping in from the outer edges threatening to envelope everything in darkness.

Why did this always have to happen? Why couldn't I just be normal for one fucking night? I was on a date with a man that I really liked and I couldn't even enjoy myself. I hated my life.

I stood from the table and excused myself to the restroom, hoping that a few minutes alone would help me to calm myself down. "I'll be right back. I just have to go to the ladies room."

The concern from earlier returned to Jordan's face when he stood with me. Breathing was becoming more difficult with each passing second and an uncontrollable sweat had broken out on my skin. Just a few more steps and I could close myself in a stall and get myself together. Just a few more steps and I would be able to freak out in private.

I didn't make it.

The sound of dishes crashing to the floor sent my panic attack into overdrive. As the glass broke on the ground, I hunched down and covered my ears as I let out a scream. My body started trembling and there was nothing I could do to stop it.

Before I could even register what was happening, I felt myself being lifted up and carried through the restaurant only to have the cool, night air hit my face moments later causing me to shake even harder.

Jordan didn't put my feet on the ground until we made it to the valet. He reached for the parking slip and quickly handed it over before turning back to me. He hunched down so we were at eye level and placed his hands on my cheeks. "Are you okay? Should I take you to the hospital or something?" he asked in a panic. "Tell me how I can help, Taylor." he asked. His eyes were wide and some of the color had washed from his complexion. He looked so worried that I couldn't stop the tears that started running down my cheeks. My first date ever and it was an epic fail. I didn't think there was a chance for there to be a worse date in the history of dates.

The shaking had started to subside and the panic quickly became overshadowed by utter humiliation. I sniffled and tried to stop my tears as I nodded my head slightly.

"You sure?" His hands slid from my cheeks and came to rest gently on the sides of my neck.

"Yes," I said past the lump that had formed in my throat.

I wasn't sure whether he believed me or not, but he dropped his hands from my neck and stood to his full height. "Okay, I'll be right back. I promise."

He turned and headed back into the restaurant, instantly being swallowed up in the sea of people as I stood there alone. I waited for the valet to come back with Jordan's car feeling like I'd just ruined the only chance I'd ever have at something normal. Another shiver passed through my body—an after effect of the panic attack—just as Jordan walked back out onto the sidewalk. He walked up beside me and removed his suit jacket, placing it over my shoulders. "Here, you're still shaking." He pulled the lapels close together and began rubbing the sides of my arms in an effort to warm me up. His gentleness was almost too much to handle and a few more rogue tears escaped and made tracks down my cheeks.

We just stood in silence as we waited as the valet pulled Jordan's car around. He opened the door and helped me in then tipped the man before making his way around the front to the driver side. We both remained silent as Jordan navigated his way through traffic. I couldn't help but soak in the crushing sorrow that was threatening to swallow me as I thought about how this was probably going to be the last time I would ever see Jordan. It didn't matter how hard I tried, I was never going to be normal.

"I'm sorry," I finally whispered in defeat.

Jordan

I felt like such an asshole. Judging by her shaking hands and her unsteady breathing, the woman that was sitting in the car next to me just experienced something that must have been terrifying for her and because I was the jackass who didn't stop to see if she had a problem, she got to experience it in front of a hundred people.

And to top it all off, she apologized.

To *me*.

I was the one that should have apologized, but I'd been wracking my brain trying to come up with something I could say to make her feel better. I had clearly taken too long and she probably thought I was pissed at having to bail out on dinner early. She couldn't have been more wrong.

I took my eyes off the road for a second to glance over at her and the sight tore at my heart. She sat wrapped in my jacket with her shoulders slumped down and her gorgeous hair obstructing my view of her face. I wanted to pull the car over just so I could pull her into my lap and wrap my arms around her. The pain she was feeling was evident in how she held herself. I needed to know who the hell put it there so I could beat the ever-loving shit out of them.

"You have nothing to apologize for," I finally replied.

Her voice was so low I barely heard her over the sounds of the engine. "I ruined our date."

I couldn't handle not seeing her face so I reached across the console and put my finger under her chin, forcing her to look at me. "Hey," I said gently. "You didn't ruin anything. When you told me you were uncomfortable in crowded places I should have gotten you out of there. I knew something was wrong and I shouldn't have ignored it."

She let out a heavy sigh and shook her head. "This is why I've never dated."

That shocked me. I knew she was speaking more to herself that to me but I had to ask. "What do you mean, never dated?" I questioned. "Like, you hardly go on dates or you've never been on one before tonight?"

She blushed, and seeing it did what it always does, it made me want to kiss her. "This was supposed to be my first date," she replied and I could hear the embarrassment in her voice.

"I find that hard to believe, Crimson. You're a beautiful woman. Men have probably gone out of their minds trying to get your attention."

She let out a laugh at that but there was no humor behind it. "I'm a mess, Jordan. Didn't you see that tonight? No guy has ever wanted to put up with my shit before, and I'm sure that after tonight, you'll be running as fast as you can in the other direction too."

That did it. I couldn't listen to her beat herself down any longer. I pulled my car over, quickly exited the freeway and pulled into the parking lot of a gas station so I could give her my undivided attention. I needed to make her see how wrong she was and I couldn't do that while I was driving.

"What are you doing?" A twinge of panic laced her words as she looked around the brightly lit parking lot.

"I need to talk to you and I need to see your face while I do."

"Please, Jordan. Can you just take me home so we can both forget what a disaster tonight was?" I couldn't stand to hear her so defeated.

Not a chance in hell.

"Taylor, I need you to listen to what I'm about to say and I need those beautiful eyes on me when I say it so I know you understand me."

Those sad amber colored eyes hit mine and the sorrow in them just about crushed me. "First of all, you are not a mess and if any of those guys didn't want to deal with something as minor as a panic attack, then…well, they're fucking idiots and their loss is clearly my gain because I'm not running anywhere."

She shook her head again in disagreement. "It's not some minor thing, Jordan. Those stupid attacks pretty much dictate my whole life. I can't even let myself get close to people because of what goes on in my head."

I knew I wasn't getting the full story, but I wasn't going to push. I wanted…no, I *needed* her to trust me. I was drawn to her in a way I'd never been drawn to another woman in my life and I needed her to see that I wasn't going anywhere.

"How long have you had to deal with this?" I asked.

She reached up and started fiddling with that locket again. I noticed she did that every time she got uncomfortable. "It started when I was seven," she finally answered.

Shit.

That was a long time to have to deal with something like that.

"Didn't your parents ever get you any help?"

She let out a small huff and rolled her eyes like the question I just asked was completely ridiculous. "They pretty much had the same opinion of me as everyone else."

"And what opinion is that?"

"That I'm a freak," she stated matter-of-factly.

It took a lot of energy not to throw the car into drive and drive all the way to Connecticut and kick their asses. "No offense, but your parents are assholes."

She laughed at that. Not a sarcastic laugh but a real one that showed off her beautiful smile. "That's something you and I can agree on."

"And you aren't a freak."

Her laughter stopped at that and I would have given anything to get it back.

"I didn't exactly have a normal childhood, Jordan. When all the kids in your school watch you have a meltdown in the middle of class you kind of get a reputation. And trust me, that stays with a person."

I didn't say anything in response; just let her tell me as much as she was willing to. If she wanted to vent and use me as the outlet, I was more than happy to accept that job.

"After that first time the kids started avoiding me, even some of the teachers would look at me funny. My dad's in politics so my parents were only really concerned with how my panic attacks would affect his chances of being re-elected."

"The panic attacks started getting worse, especially in crowded places. So it only made sense that I'd have them at school. Eventually, the kids went from avoiding me to making fun of me. I begged my parents to take me out and asked my mom if she would home school me but that would have cut into the time she could spend sipping martinis at the country club so they made me stay." I could see how difficult it was for her to admit that to me so I stayed silent and let her continue.

"Things never really got better. Eventually, I stopped trying to fit in and used all my energy trying to blend into the background. I never went to any school functions, like dances. I never attended a football or baseball game. I wasn't asked to prom. I was just...alone."

She wasn't looking at me as she spoke. Her eyes were trained out the windshield but I didn't think she was really seeing anything. She seemed to be stuck in the past as she recounted her childhood. She stayed silent for a long time before coming back to reality and turning her eyes back to me. "That's why I moved away as soon as I turned eighteen. My parents were ecstatic that they didn't have to deal with their socially awkward child anymore. They were more than happy to sign the papers to release my trust and get rid of me. Their accountant deposits a check into my bank account each month...you know...as extra incentive for me to stay away, and trust me, I'm more than happy to never speak to either of them for the rest of my life."

I didn't realize the death grip I had on the steering wheel until her eyes cut over to my hands and her eyebrows scrunched down, marring her beautiful face. I quickly flexed my fingers to get the blood pumping back through them. All the while my heart was breaking for her after everything she'd just said. How anyone could treat her with anything other than love and kindness was beyond me. Did those people not see what I did? Did they not see her beauty? Not only the beauty on the outside, but the beauty that clearly ran soul deep. If I ever ran into anyone from her past I could guarantee their funeral would have to be a closed casket. She wasn't a freak. She was a survivor. Her childhood had been shit. Her life had been shit but she'd picked herself back up. She'd moved away from all of the toxic people in her life and started over all by herself. That was commendable. As far as I could see, she was nothing short of amazing.

Then it hit me. I knew exactly what to do to make our date up to her. I was going to make sure I saw that smile again before the night was over, and if she'd let me, I knew I'd spend even longer doing whatever I could to make sure it stayed there.

I turned in my seat and put the car into gear. I had my plan. I just needed to put it into action. It was time to make her see just how special she truly was.

"Come on. Let's get out of here."

Taylor

I didn't know what possessed me to dump all of my drama on Jordan, but once I started talking, I couldn't stop. For one small second it felt nice to get everything off my chest…well, almost everything. It was kind of cleansing. That was until he put the car in gear and pulled out of the parking lot. The date had finally come to an end and all I wanted to do was go home to my empty apartment, crawl into bed and cry until I was so exhausted there was no chance of having another nightmare.

I stared out the window, letting the depression sink in as we made our way through the city. I was so wrapped up in my own thoughts that I hadn't even noticed he wasn't heading in the direction of my apartment. "Where are we going?"

I glanced over and saw a smile tugging at the corner of his mouth. "I have a surprise for you."

"Another one?" I asked, leery of his plans since the first surprise hadn't turned out so well.

"This one will be good, I promise."

A few minutes later he pulled into a packed parking lot. I wasn't sure where we were, but I couldn't help but wonder what he had up his sleeve. When I looked out my window to see where we were bright lights shone from a few yards away. Jordan hopped out of the car and I heard the back hatch open for a few seconds before he shut it and came around to the passenger door.

"Ready?" he asked, holding out his hand to me. I was hesitant but I placed my hand in his anyway and let him lead me from the car and across the parking lot.

When I finally saw where he was taking me my back went straight and I planted my feet. He turned to look at me and all I could do was shake my head furiously. "Jordan, I can't…"

He pulled me closer to his body and ran a finger gently down my cheek. "Do you trust me?" he asked. His voice had dipped low and there was a huskiness in his tone. He was so sincere.

I did. It was strange considering how short a time I'd known him, but I did. I trusted him completely. More than I had ever trusted another person.

I looked over at the high school baseball field full of people watching the kids in the middle of a game before turning back to face him. I nodded my head, and at my admission of trust, a huge smile spread across his face, highlighted by those dimples and perfect lips. I'd never wanted to kiss someone so badly.

I started walking again, but when I headed in the direction of the field entrance, I felt a tug on my hand. When I turned and looked at Jordan he tilted his head to the side indicating we were going the other way. I followed him around the side of the field just outside the fence, wondering the whole time where he was leading me.

"Where are we going?" I finally asked when curiosity got the best of me.

We walked a little further before he came to a stop and shook out the blanket that he'd been holding under his arm. I'd been so focused on where we were that I hadn't even noticed that was what he'd taken from the back of the car. He spread it on the ground and reached for my hand to help me sit down. We were facing the baseball field with a perfect view of the game going on in front of us. It was like we were a part of it but not quite. He took me to a perfect spot where were able to see and still be a part of the action, but were still at a distance far enough from the crowd of cheering people that I was able to feel safe and relaxed.

"I'll be right back," he stated before jogging away without a backward glance. I watched as he disappeared around the front of the field. Once he was out of sight I turned to watch the game playing out in front of me.

A few minutes later, Jordan returned with his arms full and a bright smile on his face. "Here," he said, leaning down so I could take some of the items from him.

"What is all this?" I asked with a laugh.

"Popcorn, sodas, hotdogs and the pièce de résistance," he said as he shook a yellow box in his hands. "Milk Duds." He sat next to me, unwrapped a hotdog and handed it to me along with a few condiment packets. I didn't get to eat any of my dinner at the restaurant and I didn't realize until that moment how hungry I actually was. I dove right in like I hadn't eaten in days, devouring the hotdog and going straight for the popcorn.

When I looked up at Jordan, I saw him grinning at me.

"What?" I asked around a mouthful of popcorn.

He chuckled and shook his head. "Nothing. You're just adorable is all."

Cue the blush.

"So you want to tell me what this is?" I indicated with a swipe of my hand toward to field.

"I thought it was kind of obvious," he replied. "See that tiny, white ball that guy over there is holding? That's called a baseball."

"Oh. He thinks he's funny," I said, laughing at his playfulness.

He gave me a shy smile before lowering his head and looking almost unsure. "You said you never got to go to a baseball game in high school. It seemed like you felt like you'd missed out on a lot of things when you told me about your childhood earlier so I wanted to try and give that to you."

I felt tears building up and blinked rapidly to keep them at bay. He was unbelievable. He'd known me less than a week, and in one night, he had already done more for me than anyone else had in twenty-three years. He took me to a high school baseball game because I'd never been to one. Not only that but he had set up a private little spot away from the other people to make sure I was able to enjoy it fully. I knew at that moment exactly how easy it would be to fall for him.

The uneasiness remained on his face as I just stared at him. He fidgeted with the collar of his shirt and cleared his throat. "Will you say something? I'm kind of having trouble reading your reaction."

I opened my mouth and snapped it closed again. I struggled to find the right words to express how amazing he made me feel. "I just…I can't…" I shook my head trying to come to grips with what he'd done. "No one has ever done anything like this for me."

I didn't give him a chance to respond. Before I could even think it through, I wrapped my arms around his neck and smashed my lips against his. He sat frozen for a few seconds before his body relaxed against mine and he returned the kiss.

I'd never kissed a guy before so I let him take the lead and allowed myself to follow, gratefully absorbing the feel of his lips against mine. When his tongue dipped out and ran across my lower lip my mouth opened on a gasp. Jordan took that as an opportunity to deepen the kiss. I swallowed his moan and his arms wrapped around my waist, pulling me closer so that I was straddling his lap as the kiss went to a whole new level. There was a desperation that was intoxicating. I was consumed by it. My hands went from the back of his neck to his hair and I grabbed hold of the blond strands, relishing the soft texture of it as I ran my fingers through its silkiness.

God, this man did things to me. When we pulled back we were both breathing heavily. We'd been so wrapped up in each other that all of the other people at the field had disappeared. He rested his forehead against mine as we tried to steady our breathing. "Christ, Taylor. I'd love nothing more than to keep making out with you, but this isn't really the place for it."

I instantly realized we were in the middle of a high school campus surrounded by students. I couldn't contain the laugh that bubbled up when I realized that we'd just been making out like teenagers while surrounded by teenagers.

It took me several seconds to get my laughter under control, and when I finally did and turned to look at Jordan, he was smiling at me affectionately. "There it is," he whispered as he trailed his thumb across my lower lip.

"What?"

"That smile. I've been dying to put that smile back on your beautiful face all night."

I turned my cheek into his palm and soaked up his affection. "Thank you for putting it back."

He pressed his lips back to mine in a somewhat chaste kiss. "I'm starting to think there isn't much of anything I wouldn't do to see you smile."

Yeah, I was definitely in danger of falling for Jordan Donovan.

We spent the rest of the evening cuddled up together on the blanket. I sat between his thighs with my back resting against his chest as he trailed his fingers up and down my arms. The date went from being an epic fail to the best date in the history of dates. And it was all because of Jordan.

He'd given me normal. Even if it was for just one night.

I was hit with an unexpected sense of disappointment when Jordan pulled his car in front of my apartment building. I'd had so much fun that I didn't want the night to end.

Staring up at the glass and steel structure, I made a decision that had butterflies exploding in my belly. He'd made me feel normal for the first time and all I could think was that I wanted that feeling to continue.

I looked over at Jordan and admired his attractive profile as he put the car in park.

It was now or never.

I reached for my locket and started rubbing a circle with my thumb. "Uh…do you want to come up?" I asked nervously.

His face lit up and all my nerves disappeared. That expression told me all I needed to know. He wanted the night to continue just as badly as I did.

"Yeah. I'd like that."

He hopped out of the car and came around to collect me from the passenger seat. I started walking toward the building when Jordan gave my hand a tug and pulled me back into his solid frame. I tilted my face up to meet his gaze, and as soon as I did, his lips came down on mine in a kiss so hungry I felt my knees give out. He wrapped one arm around my waist to hold me up and plunged his free hand into my hair, tugging just enough to cause a moan to break loose from my throat.

After several seconds he pulled back slightly and traced the tip of his tongue across my bottom lip. "I've been dying to do that since we left the ball park," he whispered against my lips.

Shyly, I pulled back and reached for his hand, lacing our fingers together and led him into my building. As we made our way to the elevator Gary looked up from his book—*The Shining* this time—and shot me a knowing grin. "Nice evening, Taylor?" he asked cheekily.

I felt the heat creeping up my neck and face as Jordan wrapped an arm around my shoulder. I could feel his body shaking with silent laughter.

"Yes, Gary. Thank you. It was fantastic."

The corners of his mouth tipped up a little more and I heard him mumble, "I bet," as he looked back down at his book.

When we got into the privacy of the elevator Jordan pulled me to him, wrapped both arms around my waist and gave me a peck on the lips. "I think I kind of like that guy."

I smiled against his lips and replied, "I kind of like him too."

We stayed wrapped around each other until the elevator opened on my floor. I had twenty floors to decide exactly how I was going to make a move on Jordan and I'd come up with nothing. Not a single damn thing.

My hands were shaking so much that I had trouble getting the key in the lock. Seeing my tenseness, Jordan placed his hand over mine and gently guided the key into the lock. I finally got my door unlocked and open with his help. I turned the lights on and dropped my purse on the entryway table. My palms started sweating again and I had to rub them on my dress as I turned back to face him. "Um…do you want something to drink? I have water, soda…oh! I might have a bottle of wine or some beer or something…" Now that he was in my apartment, I didn't have a clue what I was going to do. I'd spent so much of my life avoiding other people that I'd never even been with a man before. I'd had a taste of what it was like to be normal because of Jordan and I desperately wanted more. I wanted to be with him.

"Sure, whatever you're having is fine."

I was definitely having something stronger than water; I was going to need it. I opened the fridge, grabbed two beers and handed one to him before opening the other and taking a long pull.

Oh God, I don't think I can do this.

I turned my back on him and rested my hands on the island trying to calm my nerves when I felt the hair being brushed off the back of my neck. His breath tickled against my bare skin. My head fell to the side to allow better access. "You know, we don't have to do anything if you're not ready," he whispered.

With just the brush of his nose against the shell of my ear, he'd eradicated all of my anxiety. Overwhelmed by what he was doing to my body, I spun around and kissed him. I poured every ounce of need I had for him into that kiss. My head started spinning when his tongue dove into my mouth and tangled with mine. He tasted like mint and a hint of beer; it was absolutely intoxicating.

I melted further into the kiss when he trailed his hands down my waist, past my ass and to the back of my thighs. Using those delectable muscles, he lifted me off the ground and wrapped both of my legs around his lean hips as he hoisted me up and planted my ass on the island.

On instinct, my nails raked lightly down Jordan's back as his lips left mine and glided down my neck to my collarbone.

There was no way of holding back the moan that escaped. "Oh God, Jordan."

"Bedroom, baby," he said into my neck. "Where is it?"

I needed him. Now.

"Down the hall," I flung my arm carelessly in the direction of my room and before I could register his movements I was lifted back up and being carried out of the kitchen and into the bedroom like I weighed nothing.

I had no clue what I was doing but I gladly let Jordan take the lead again. I wanted him more than my next breath. The fear of what I was about to do was drowned out by my overwhelming desire for him. Even if I had been second guessing myself earlier, it was pointless now. I was lost in Jordan's touch, unable to see anything but him.

I felt him kick the bedroom door open and we stumbled in. Just as I thought he was about to drop me, he turned and landed on my bed on his back with me on top, straddling his hips. I kept kissing him as he sat up and reached around the back of my dress and started patting around for what I could only assume was the zipper.

Laughter bubbled up when he let out a frustrated growl and ripped his mouth from mine. "Where's the fucking zipper on this damn thing?" he said, practically spinning me around on his lap so he could find it.

I couldn't stop it; he was just so damn frustrated that it was funny as hell. The laugh I'd been trying to suppress came out in a snort and there was no stopping it once it started. "It's on the side," I wheezed out.

He turned me back around and looked up at me with amusement in his eyes. "I'm so glad this is funny for you. I'm going out of my head trying to get you naked and you're cracking up."

I snorted again. "I'm sorry! I'm so sorry…but you should see your face. It's hilarious!"

I could feel his body shake as he began to chuckle along with me. "I'm just going to rip the damn thing off."

"No!" I shouted as I hopped off his lap. "It's the only dress I own."

He stood and stalked after me like a lion stalked its prey. His normally light hazel eyes had grown dark with lust; seeing him so turned on made it difficult to breathe. "I'll buy you a new one," he hissed as he lunged at me. I let out a startled screech as he lifted me up and threw me onto the bed. Before I could blink, the dress was gone and I was lying there in nothing but pale blue lace panties and a matching bra.

I felt my entire body turning red as his eyes scanned over every inch of bare flesh. I lifted my arms in an attempt to cover myself but Jordan grabbed hold of my wrists, his eyes hitting mine. "Don't do that. Please don't cover yourself around me." The lust that had been in his eyes seconds earlier disappeared and had been replaced by something deeper…something I didn't quite recognize. "You're so fucking perfect," he whispered as he leaned over me and pressed his lips to the center of my chest.

I never thought anyone would ever say those words to me. I was the complete opposite of perfect, but the passion in his voice made me want to believe him. It felt as if everything with Jordan was moving at warp speed, but it all seemed so familiar, almost natural. His voice, his touch, how he looked at me, all of those things broke down my barriers and erased any doubt I might have had.

I sighed against his lips and realized I was at a complete disadvantage. There I was, lying underneath him practically naked, while he was still fully clothed. I reached for his shirt and started working the buttons but the tremble in my hands made the task nearly impossible. "I need to see you," I said in a frantic plea, barely recognizing my voice. "Please, Jordan." The man had reduced me to begging after just one date. Either he was that good or I was just that desperate. I hoped it was the former.

"Anything you want, baby." He sat back on his haunches, still hovering above me and made quick work of the buttons on his shirt. As he pulled it from his slacks, his abs flexed and his biceps bulged as he stripped it off. It was official. Jordan Donovan was a freaking Adonis. No man on earth should ever look that good.

His body was a work of art.

I sat up and trailed my tongue along his ribs, my body reacting instinctively.

"*Christ*," he ground out before covering my body with his. Reaching behind me, he flicked the clasp of my bra and pulled it down my arms without ever breaking away from the kiss. I arched my back, pushing my chest into his as close as I could. I felt like my body would spontaneously combust at any moment if he didn't touch me. As if reading exactly what my body needed, he cupped one of my breasts and rubbed his thumb across its peak while his mouth wrapped around the other. My hips bucked under his as he sucked my nipple into his mouth. I fisted my hands in his hair and let out a needy groan in response to his teeth scraping against my aching tip.

"Jordan, please," I begged, still not quite sure what I was begging for. My body knew what it wanted even if my brain wasn't catching on. And I was hungry for it.

Desperate for it.

His hand on my breast started down my waist while his lips made their way back to mine. "I've got you, baby," he said into my mouth just as his fingers slipped past the edge of my panties. I let out a gasp as he slid one finger through my wetness before pulling back to circle around my clit. My breathing became frantic and I grabbed hold of the comforter, fisting it in both hands so tightly I was sure I'd rip it.

"So wet," he mumbled as he pushed one finger into me, pumping it in and out so slowly I wanted to scream. When he began to insert a second finger I felt a flicker of pain as he began to stretch me. "Jesus baby, you're so fucking tight."

I couldn't tell him the truth…that I was a virgin. I didn't want to risk him stopping if he found out so I did what came naturally, I lied. "It's been a while," I replied as I pulled his mouth back to mine and wrapped my tongue around his. His hands continued to do glorious things to my body. "Please," I pleaded. "Jordan, I need you."

"What do you need, baby? I'll give you anything, just say the words."

"I need you inside me," I gasped.

Before I could process his movement, Jordan removed his hand from between my legs and jumped off the bed. He reached for his wallet, removed a square foil packet, tossed it on the floor and ripped his slacks and boxer briefs down his body in one quick motion.

Holy shit.

In that very moment I started to re-think everything about my plan. All I could do was lay there and stare at Jordan in all his naked glory as he rolled the condom down his long, thick shaft. There was *no way in hell* this was going to work.

He must have read the look on my face correctly because he said, "Don't worry, it'll fit. You're body was made for mine."

He hooked one arm around the back of my thigh and pushed it up closer to my chest as he poised himself at my entrance. I closed my eyes and tilted my head back waiting for him to move but he wasn't having that. "Look at me, Taylor. Never take your eyes off mine." There was so much intensity in his voice that my eyes flew open and locked on his, immediately being pulled into the lust that swam in them.

He thrust forward just slightly and hissed out a breath. "*Fuck,*" he moaned before pulling back and pushing in a little further. "You're so damn tight," he panted. "Am I hurting you?"

"No," It was the second time in minutes that I had lied. The truth was that the burning sensation was becoming almost too much to take as he pulled out and pushed back in slowly, only sliding in a fraction of an inch further each time. "Just do it, Jordan," I demanded, praying the pain wouldn't be so intense if he just got it over with and slid all the way in.

His hips pulled back and he pounded all the way in with one deep thrust...and I instantly regretted my decision. I let out a sharp scream and hot tears blurred my vision then started rolling down the corner of my eyes. The burning sensation intensified to a horrible level and I felt like he was tearing me in two.

"Jesus fucking Christ!" he bellowed into my neck where he'd buried his head the minute he was fully seating inside me. He didn't move as he attempted to get his breathing under control.

He attempted to pull out, but I whimpered at the slight movement and dug my nails into the skin on his back. His pulling out hurt almost as much as when he pushed in. He lifted his head and looked at my with what appeared to be a combination of concern and anger.

I tried to wiggle out from under him but it just hurt too damn much. "Be still," he demanded. "You're going to make it worse. Just...just try and relax."

The tears trickling down the sides of my face were no longer from the pain, but instead, from humiliation. I'd lied to him. I'd kept the fact that I was a virgin from him, and now that he knew, I just wanted to curl into a tiny little ball and fade away.

I tried to turn my face to the side and cover it with my hands but he wouldn't let me. Pinning both my wrists in one hand above my head, he used his other hand to turn my face back to his. "Why didn't you tell me, baby?"

"Because I was afraid you'd stop," I said in a strangled voice.

I tried to give his body a shove, but he refused to move; he just pinned me deeper into the mattress. "I wouldn't have stopped," he finally whispered catching me totally off guard.

"You wouldn't have?" I asked with a sniffle.

He leaned down and placed a kiss on my mouth. "Fuck no. I've wanted you like crazy from the moment I laid eyes on you. There's no way I could ever say no to you…but I would have done things differently. I could have made it less painful but you didn't give me that option."

I sniffled again and tried to wipe the tears away with the back of my hands. He gently brushed the hair off my face and gave me a sympathetic smile. "Do you trust me?" he asked for the second time that night.

"Yes."

"Then let me take care of you, okay? I promise I won't hurt you again." He leaned back down and kissed me so fiercely it made my toes curl. His fingers made their way back between my legs and he started circling that tight bundle of nerves again, eliciting a deep moan from me. "That's it, baby," he said against my lips.

His fingers sped up and his hips started to thrust slowly. The pain that was there earlier was gone, a dull ache the only thing that remained.

"Jordan," I gasped as I raised my hips to meet his. His thrusts became faster and deeper as he continued to kiss me. He released his hold on my leg and I wrapped them both around his hips, digging my heels into his back. My arms made their way around his neck and we both began to move faster. I felt my release building up inside me again as Jordan powered in and out. Sweat broke out on our skin as our thrusts became frantic and I was lost. I couldn't think. All I could do was feel. Feel Jordan's strong hands on me, feel him moving inside me, feel all the emotions he stirred up that I hadn't realized even existed. "I need you," I cried out, unable to hold back the words.

"I'm right here, baby." His eyes were on mine, never wavering; the intensity was almost enough to push me over. "Let go, Taylor. I've got you."

That was all it took. Those few words pushed me over the edge and I came, crying out his name over and over. Overwhelmed, tears ran down the sides of my cheeks.

"Christ, baby…so good," he groaned before burying his face in my neck as he followed me over seconds later.

We were both breathing hard and all of the energy was drained from my body. I was blissfully exhausted and on the edge of sleep when I felt Jordan brush the hair away from my neck and tug my earlobe with his teeth. "Perfect," I heard him whisper right before I drifted off completely.

It was just a dream…It was just a dream. I chanted over and
over in my head as I tried to forget what I'd seen. Tried to
forget that horrible poem running on repeat in my head. I'd
woken up from my nightmare screaming as the knife was
plunged into my stomach but like always, I was alone in my
bed, no killer lurking in the shadows.

That was when it hit me. I was alone in my bed.

Alone.

When I'd fallen asleep last night my cheek had been
resting on Jordan's strong chest and our legs were tangled
together, but as I looked around the sun filled room, he was
nowhere to be found. There were no signs that he'd ever even
been there, and if it wasn't for the dull throb between my
thighs, I might have been concerned that I imagined the whole
thing.

He left.

The thought caused tears to prick the backs of my eyes,
but I inhaled deeply and blinked them away. I had been
nothing more than a one-night stand.

But…why?

Why would he bother saying all of those wonderful things
to me if he had known he was just going to walk away
afterwards? I felt a knot deep in my stomach as I recalled all of
the things he'd said the night before. I felt like such an idiot for
dropping my guard and allowing myself to buy into everything
he said.

I could spend hours wracking my brain trying to come up
with answers, but it was useless. He was a guy and that's what
guys did. At least I'd gotten a few hours of freedom from the
darkness thanks to him. I'd felt like a normal person for a small
amount of time so I tried to concentrate on being thankful to

Jordan for that. I needed to ignore the pain twisting in my gut at the realization that I obviously meant less than nothing.

Glancing at the clock, I noticed that I only had an hour before my shift started. No time for yoga in an attempt to rid my mind of the horrible dream or of Jordan.

I stood from my bed and was hit with blinding pain. I grabbed the sides of my head as the migraine caused me to double over onto the floor. It was another hallucination. No...*vision*. I caught flashes of blonde hair and screams. Then I remembered what Daniel told me. If I tried to embrace the visions the headaches would stop.

I had a decision to make. I could either accept that this was my life, and I could try to help the people that I saw, or I could ignore it and...I didn't even want to consider the outcome of that decision.

I pushed myself up and into sitting pose that I'd learned from years of yoga and tried to breathe through the pain that threatened to overrun me. Inhaling through my nose and exhaling through my mouth, I attempted to clear my mind and see the woman who was running in terror.

The pain began to subside as I concentrated on opening up and embracing what I was seeing. The image became clearer and I could make out more details than I could the first time, but I still couldn't see her face.

I'd done what Daniel asked so why couldn't I see her face?

Her fear was coursing through me and a cold sweat broke out across my skin. The pain in my head had disappeared completely the harder I concentrated, but the woman never turned around. And just as quickly as the vision came, it was gone.

I didn't understand. I did everything I was supposed to do. I embraced the vision and I still couldn't see who the woman was. There was nothing I could do to help her if I wasn't able to find out who she was.

I needed to find Daniel.

I needed answers.

//

The Past

"Do you have any clue how special you are, my sweet Lydia?" Granny asked as she clasped her locket around my neck. "You're just like me, love. We have a special gift."

It was the night before my seventh birthday and my parents actually allowed my grandmother to come for a short visit. They had told her she wasn't allowed at the party because she couldn't be trusted not to make a scene, but I was happy just to have time alone with her. My mom said Granny was crazy and hardly let me see her, so on the rare occasions it was allowed, I wanted her all to myself.

"What special gift, Granny?" I asked as I stretched across my bed and laid my head in her lap. We always did that. I would lay my head in her lap and she would run her fingers through my hair over and over until I finally fell asleep. My mom never played with my hair the way Granny did.

"We can see things, sweet girl. Special things that no one else can see. We have visions," she whispered with a smile. "And it's our job to try and help those we see in our visions."

I turned my head and looked up at her face. "I don't understand. What do you mean help those we see?"

"My dear Lydia," she whispered as she ran the back of her knuckles down my cheek. "The things that we see aren't always easy. They can be scary but you have to stay strong. Do you understand?"

I nodded up at her even though I didn't.

"You have to be strong, Lydia. Don't let the visions scare you to the point you won't allow yourself to help those who need it. Always remember that this is a gift. It won't always seem like it, but I promise it is."

"Will you be here to help me?"

She gave me a sad smile and I saw the tears forming in her eyes. "I wish I could, darling. I'd give anything to help you through this but you know I can't."

She was right. I already knew my mother wouldn't allow it.

I felt a tear run down my cheek as I wrapped my little fingers around my grandmother's locket. "I'm scared. I don't want to see things that will frighten me, Granny."

"Shhh," she soothed. "You are strong, sweet girl," she whispered. "So much stronger than you know."

Granny had been wrong about me.

I wasn't strong. If I had been strong I wouldn't have ignored my gift and let innocent people die just because I was scared. I could have stopped it. That's what the gift was for, to stop innocent people from dying, but I'd been weak and let my fear keep me from doing what I was meant to do.

I was still scared, I didn't think I'd ever stop being scared but I had no choice. It was either live with it or die…and despite how shitty my life had been, I wasn't ready to die just yet. The first twenty-three years sucked but I was determined to make the next twenty-three worth it.

I'd had a taste of what life could be like, and I'd loved it. If I could just stop living in constant fear day in and day out, I would be happy. It turned out Jordan wasn't the one for me, but if I could move past what I had allowed to hold me back all my life, then maybe I would open myself up to the chance that there could be someone else.

I was going to take back my life. I made a promise to my grandmother all those years ago and I needed to keep it. I could only hope I wasn't too late.

As I got ready for my shift at Benny's, I kept hoping that Daniel would show up to tell me what to do. I needed help and he was the only one that could help me. He was my Guide after all and I was going to make damn sure he guided me.

The breakfast rush came and went with no signs of Daniel. Every time the door opened I looked to see if it was him coming through it but it never was. I was starting to become disheartened at the thought of him not showing. I'd gone from having no men in my life to having two that I couldn't count on when I needed them most. Daniel was doing a shitty job as my Guide and Jordan was just an asshole. My mood went from hopeful to sour before lunch and unfortunately everyone noticed.

"I think you're about to wipe a hole right through that table, Taylor," Cassie said from over my shoulder.

"Huh?" I was so busy concentrating on how much Jordan and Daniel sucked that I wasn't even paying attention to what Cassie was saying.

"Umm," she mumbled. "So…how was your date?" I let out a *pfft* sound and went back to scrubbing the already sparkling table. "That good, huh?" She placed a consolatory hand on my shoulder. "Want to talk about it?"

I turned and slumped against the table in defeat as I looked up at her in all her glossy haired, model skinny glory. "It was a little rocky in the beginning…" I started then gave that statement a little more thought. "Actually, it totally bombed."

"What happened?" she asked with rapt attention as she twirled a lock of her shiny hair around her perfectly manicured finger.

Cassie didn't know the details about all the issues I had but she did know one thing. I let out a sigh and dropped my head. "I had a panic attack in the middle of the restaurant."

"Oh sweetie." She wrapped her arms around me and squeezed a little too tightly.

"I know," I breathed out once she released me. "It was so embarrassing…but then he was so damn sweet and totally made up for everything. I don't know what happened."

I told her all about spilling my guts to Jordan about my childhood and how he surprised me by taking me to the ball game.

"Well, how did he act when he dropped you off?" she asked.

My skin instantly heated up and I realized I'd backed myself into a corner. Instead of answering, I walked past her and started wiping down another table as if my life depended on it. I heard her let out a squeal and when I turned to look at her she had the biggest shit-eating grin spread across her lips. "You little ho...you totally had sex with him, didn't you?"

I looked around the diner, frantically hoping no one overheard her before I grabbed her arm and dragged her to the back office. She laughed the whole way.

"A first date lay...I didn't think you had it in you, honey." I knew I had to have been three shades of red but that didn't stop her. "I've got to say, babe, I'm looking at you in a whole new light. How was it? Please tell me he's as good as I imagine he is, because I'm painting a pretty vivid picture in my head right now."

I reached for my locket and started fiddling. "Uh...well...at first it hurt like you wouldn't believe, but then it got better and..."

She jumped in and interrupted me, "Whoa, he's that big?" she asked with wide, amazed eyes.

"Um...I don't really have anything to compare it to but I'm pretty sure he'd be considered big."

And...there it was.

I saw the realization of what I was saying cross her face just before her jaw hit the floor. "Taylor, you were a virgin?" she whispered like she was asking if I'd just committed a crime.

I crossed my arms over my chest and went on the defensive. "Well you don't have to say it like that. I'm only twenty-three. It's not *that* unheard of."

"Oh, no, Sweetie, I didn't mean it like that." The regret at her choice of words washed over her features and she sounded so sincere that I couldn't stay mad at her.

"It's okay," I muttered.

"Did he...did he know?" she asked hesitantly.

I ran my hands through my hair and gave it small tug at the roots then decided to just let it all out. "Not at first, but he kind of figured it out on his own."

Her mouth formed an "O" and she nodded her head in understanding. "It's just that the date was going so well, and you already know I'm not really like everyone else, and...well...he just made me feel...normal for once. I just wanted to keep that feeling for as long as I could.

"He was so sweet and understanding. All I wanted was one night to be a regular person, you know? He actually gave me that. But I woke up this morning and he was gone. He just...left."

I tried to blink back the tears that formed in my eyes but it was pointless; they fell down my cheeks anyway.

Cassie rushed to me and wrapped me in a hug, holding me there for a long while. When she finally pulled back she looked my directly in the eyes. "Let's get one thing straight, you *are* normal, Taylor. You just have a few issues. There is nothing wrong with you."

If she only knew.

"If he can't see how lucky he'd be to have you then he's an asshole who doesn't deserve to have you spit on him if he were on fire."

She spoke with so much conviction, I still had to laugh. I wiped my eyes and gave her a smile. "Thank you, Cass. You're kind of awesome."

"You're kind of awesome too, babe." We made our way out of the office and headed back to the front of the diner. "Hey, I know just what you need. I'm bartending tonight at Dark. Why don't you come see me and I'll cover your drinks for the night."

"How do you possibly have the energy to work here then go bartend at night?" I asked.

Cassie worked at Benny's Diner during the day, but most nights she bartended at one of Seattle's most popular nightclubs. It exhausted me just thinking about the hours she kept.

She shrugged then threw a wink at me from over her shoulder. "A girl's gotta do what a girl's gotta do for Jimmy Choo."

I appreciated the invitation and I felt even closer to her for being so amazing, but there was no way I'd be able to handle a packed nightclub if I couldn't even make it through dinner at a restaurant. "Thanks, Cassie, but I don't think a nightclub's the best idea right now."

She smiled knowingly and gave a small nod. "I understand. But if you ever need anything, or just want to talk I'm here, okay?"

I felt the burn of tears but for once they were for a different reason.

For once they were happy tears.

"The body of Samantha Turner was found last night near Alki Point Lighthouse," the newscaster stated.

I'd gotten home from work completely exhausted and turned on the TV to watch *The Following* when the news broke in. A flash of recognition washed over me when I saw a picture of the young, blonde haired woman flashed across the screen.

"Police say Turner, twenty-four, was reported missing five days ago when she didn't show up for work at Cherry Street Coffee House. Details are still coming in, but police confirmed a poem was found at the scene.

"As with the other victims, it is believed Turner was murdered at a different location before her body was dumped in a public area known to be a popular tourist destination. Stay tuned to KIRO, Channel Seven as more details come in."

The picture came back up on the screen and I sat forward to study Samantha Turner's face. Blonde hair, same build as the woman in my vision. Was it possible the woman on the TV was the same woman I'd seen in my vision? Had I been too late to help her?

I dropped my head into my hands. The thought that I had let another helpless person die for no reason sucked me down into the dark recesses of depression. The knowledge of what I had let happen by ignoring my visions began to wear on me; the guilt was stifling. I hated knowing I could have prevented the pain and suffering of the people that came to me in those visions. I had been too much of a coward to help.

I stood up and headed to my intercom when it rang, pulling me from my inner turmoil. "Yeah Gary?" I asked, knowing he was already on duty.

"Miss Taylor..." even though we had an agreement that I'd keep all early morning runs contained in the complex gym if Gary would stop calling me *Miss* he still insisted on formality in cases where it seemed unprofessional. "There's a gentleman here to see you."

Had Jordan actually decided to show his face after bailing out on me the night before? I stood in silence for a few seconds trying to figure out if I should tell Gary to let him up or kick his ass out of the building. Finally deciding that I wanted the pleasure of laying into him myself, I pressed the button and spoke into the intercom, "You can send him up. Thank you, Gary."

"My pleasure, Miss Taylor."

I hated that my nerves were fried at the idea of seeing Jordan again, but I couldn't stop myself from running to the bathroom to check my reflection in the mirror, making sure I looked absolutely perfect when I ripped him a new one for being the world's biggest asshole. I quickly ran a brush through my unruly hair and pinched my cheeks to add some color. I'd just finished changing out of my work shirt into a thin, cotton tank top that had seen better days but still highlighted my best assets, when there was a knock on the door.

I reached for the knob after taking a few calming breaths and swung it open.

"I've got to hand it to you; you've got balls of...Daniel?" I sputter in shock when I lifted my gaze and saw him standing there. He definitely wasn't who I planned to see standing there when I opened my door.

"Oh, please continue," he replied with a devilish smirk. "I'm dying to know what my balls are made of."

Ignoring his remark, I asked, "What are you doing here?"

His eyes drifted over my shoulder to the TV and his smirk morphed into a look of regret. "You already saw it." When he looked back at me I saw the pity in his eyes and I knew.

"It was her, wasn't it? The girl from my vision...the one I couldn't see clearly? She's the one they just found."

There wasn't a doubt in my mind that I was right but when he nodded his head something inside me broke. I walked back to the couch and collapsed, dropping my head in my hands as the tears flowed down, dripping an obscure pattern on the hard wood beneath me.

I felt the cushion next to me sink as Daniel sat down and wrapped his arms around me. After several minutes, I finally lifted my head and ran my fingers under my eyes in an attempt to wipe away any smudged mascara. "I tried, Daniel. I swear. Another vision came to me this morning and I tried so hard to see her face but I just couldn't." The last words broke on a sob and he pulled me into his warm, hard chest for comfort.

"I know, Taylor. I know. It was already too late."

I let out a frustrated sigh and shot off the couch. "Then what was the point?" I asked pacing the length of my living room. "Why see her again this morning if she was already dead? And why couldn't I see her face, Daniel? I did everything you said but I still couldn't see her."

He leaned forward, resting his elbows on his knees, and hung his head. "This gift isn't like riding a bike, Taylor. You can't just ignore it for fourteen years and expect everything to return like it should the first time out of the gate. Like anyone with a gift, you have to practice. You have to hone it."

"What if it's too late?" I said on a gasp when the reality of the situation finally hit me like a ton of bricks. "What if it never comes back and whoever the hell this higher power is that gave it to me has already decided to replace me?"

He was in front of my face before I could blink. He gripped my shoulders and gave me a small shake to pull me out of those terrible thoughts. "Hey, enough of that. It's not too late. I swear, Taylor, I'm going to do everything in my power to help you but you can't think like that, okay? Promise me."

I felt miserable and exhausted. I gave a weak nod and accepted the comfort he offered when he wrapped me in a tight embrace. There was no intimacy involved, but Daniel somehow managed to give me exactly what I needed…comfort and security. It was as if I'd known him my entire life. I felt an almost familial connection to Daniel, like I knew he would always be there to protect me and keep me on the right path when I needed it most. With his towering frame holding me up and his reassuring words in my ear, I started to feel like he was right, like I could pull through this and come out on the other side. I buried my face in his chest and returned the hug, squeezing his waist tightly as I tried to calm myself.

My mind was reeling and all I could think was that I didn't want to let anyone else down.

Jordan

I sat at my desk so exhausted it hurt to keep my eyelids open. I looked over at my partner, who appeared to be just as tired as I was, and made a decision to call it. "Go home,

Stevens. There isn't anything else we can do tonight." The clock read 9:45 and we'd been working since the call came in around 2:00 that morning. Even if we did find a lead, both of our brains were so fried it was almost guaranteed that we would screw something up.

Stevens rubbed his hands over his face roughly before letting out a frustrated grunt. "I don't fucking get it. He's escalating and we don't have shit."

I leaned as far back as my chair would allow and laced my hands behind my head. "I don't know man, and it's driving me fucking crazy. We've got four girls with nothing in common. Different hair colors, different body types, different ethnicities, different jobs. There isn't one goddamn link between any of them that we can find."

Stevens stood up and stretched his arms over his head, causing the buttons on his shirt to stretch to a dangerous level. "All I know is if I have to read one more of those twisted as fuck poems, I'm going to go fucking mental. He's one sick son of a bitch. I can't take seeing any more dead girls. This is the kind of shit that stays with a person."

I understood exactly what he was talking about. I didn't think it would ever be possible to get those girls' images out of my head. As he passed by my desk on his way out he paused and slapped me on the shoulder. "We'll get him man."

I wanted to believe that, but with each girl, my hopes dwindled a little more. After staring at the computer screen for a few more minutes, I finally gave up and started shutting everything down. I needed to get back to Taylor. I left her bed in such a rush earlier that I completely forgot to leave her a note. Every time I thought about picking up the phone and calling her something else popped up and got in the way. I was either processing the crime scene, dealing with the evidence from the crime lab, or talking to Samantha Turner's parents. That was part of the job I was never going to get used to. Having to inform the victim's loved ones that they'd lost a family member…it damaged something inside me every time I had to have that conversation, something I was afraid couldn't be repaired.

But the idea of seeing Taylor again made a day full of darkness seem just a little brighter. I just hoped she wasn't pissed about me leaving without a word this morning. She just looked so damn peaceful and I knew what I was about to walk into was going to be awful. I didn't want to expose her to that part of my life if I could somehow prevent it.

I got in my car and headed over to her apartment, stopping first to pick up some flowers just to be on the safe side. Women were finicky creatures; the only way for a man to navigate safely was to be preemptive.

"Can I help you?" the older, gray haired woman behind the counter asked when I walked in the door.

"Uh, yeah, what do you recommend I get for potentially screwing up with a woman I just started dating, but want to apologize for said potential screw up because I would very much like to continue dating her?" I asked, figuring I might as well be upfront.

She gave me a sweet smile full of humor before walking around the counter over to a refrigerated display case. "Well, roses are always a good way to get a woman to forgive you."

I looked through the glass at all the different colored roses. They were pretty but Taylor didn't seem like a roses type of woman. She was different...unique. I wanted something that represented her. I kept scanning, trying to find something that made me think of her, when I finally saw the perfect arrangement.

"What about those?" I asked, pointing to the bouquet in the middle of the case.

"Oh, good choice. That's our Gerbera Bright arrangement."

My face screwed up in confusion as I looked over at her. "Your...huh?"

She gave a small laugh and opened the display case. "Gerbera daisies dear, in five different colors. They're definitely different."

"Well, she's different," I said with a smile.

"I don't think you'll have to worry about her staying mad at you after this," she replied as she rang up the purchase.

All I could do was hope she was right.

I left the shop and quickly made my way over to Taylor's place. When I walked through the doors, I saw Gary sitting behind the desk reading. He glanced up with a smile before it quickly morphed into a look of uncertainty. "Uh…Good evening, Mr. Donovan."

"Hey Gary. How you doing tonight?"

He looked me up and down before replying, "Better than you, from the looks of it. Are you okay, sir?"

I let out a sigh and ran my free hand through my hair. "You don't want to know the half of it. Anyway, you could let me up without buzzing her? I kind of want to surprise her," I said holding up the flowers for him to see."

"Oh, I don't know…that might not be such a good idea."

I leaned against the desk and smiled. "Come on man, you'd be doing me a huge favor. You know I had to bail out of here last night in a rush. I want to make it up to her."

He quirked a brow and looked at me suspiciously. "Can't think of many reasons for a man to burn out on a beautiful young woman at two in the morning. You have to get home to your wife or something?" he asked, his tone of voice full of accusation.

I hung my head and reached into my back pocket. "Murder scene," I replied, showing my badge to the old guy.

His eyes widened at that and the suspicion disappeared. "I'm sorry, sir…"

I slid my badge back in my pocket and lifted a hand to wave off his apology. "No worries, I'd have thought the same thing. But now that you know the truth, you think you can help me out?"

I could tell he was fidgeting from behind the desk but all I cared about was getting to Taylor. "I guess," he finally relented. "But I really think I should buzz her…"

I was off toward the elevators before he could finish. "You're a saint, Gary," I called over my shoulder. "I won't forget this."

As the doors opened and I stepped in I could have sworn I heard him mumble, "Oh, I don't doubt that."

The elevator dinged and my senses went on immediate alert when I noticed the door to Taylor's apartment was cracked open. On instinct, I reached for my gun and hit nothing but air. I had made sure to take it off before coming up to Taylor's just in case guns scared her. I instantly regretted that decision. I felt the hairs on the back of my neck stand on end as I inched closer.

What I saw when I pushed the door open the rest of the way was *not* what I was expecting to see.

Taylor was standing in the middle of her living room with her arms around another man. I don't think I'd ever wanted to kill another human-being more than I did at that very moment.

"This looks cozy," I ground out. "Am I interrupting?"

Taylor dropped her arms and quickly looked my way. "Jordan? What are you doing here?"

"Well, I just thought that after having a shitty ass day I'd come see my girl." The loser standing next to her crossed his arms over his chest and glared at me. I could glare just as good as the next guy so I shot a burn-in-hell look back at him. "Who's this guy?" I asked, not taking my eyes off him.

"I don't really see how that's any of your business," the douche bag responded.

"Is that right?" I took another step into the apartment as he stepped closer to me.

"Yeah, that's right."

We were inches away from each other when Taylor stepped in between us, attempting to push us apart. "Stop!" she demanded. "You can whip your dicks out and see whose is bigger when I'm not around, but for now, this is my apartment and I'm really not in the mood to put up with a macho pissing contest."

"Your boyfriend here started it," the asshole replied.

"That's right, boyfriend," I said, pointing at my chest. "You'd do well to not fucking forget that."

"Whoa, wait just one goddamn minute," Taylor screeched. "Boyfriend? I'm not exactly an expert on this topic, but I'm pretty sure boyfriends don't disappear in the middle of the night after having sex just a few hours earlier. And I'm also pretty sure having one date doesn't constitute boyfriend status even if sex was involved…especially if a girl doesn't hear from the guy at all the next day."

"Crimson," I whispered apologetically. Our conversation would have gone so much easier if that asshole wasn't standing right next to her.

"Holy shit man, I think it's safe to say that was an epic fail on your part."

"Well no one fucking asked you!" I bellowed. "Taylor, who the hell is this guy?"

He didn't let her answer. "I'm an old friend. That's all you need to know, seeing as you'll probably be leaving in about thirty seconds."

I turned an accusing eye on Taylor. "I thought you said you left everyone from your past behind."

That motherfucker interrupted…*again*. I was seconds away from going from pissed off to nuclear if he didn't shut the hell up. "I guess you could say I'm here to make amends." He gave Taylor a loving look that made me want to knock his pretty white teeth down his throat.

"Were you two involved or something?" I forced myself to ask, dreading the answer.

The dynamic between the two of them changed as soon as the words left my mouth. "No!" both of them demanded.

"It's not like that," Taylor said at the same time the asshole spouted out, "Dude, she's like a sister to me." Neither one of them looked comfortable with the thought of being intimate and I instantly felt some of the tension seeping away.

"Daniel," she reached up and touched his arm. I wanted to rip that arm off his smug as hell body and beat the shit out of him with it. "Please just go. I'll call you later, all right?"

He put his hands on her shoulders and I seriously contemplated murder for the first time in my life. I didn't care if they said they were just friends; he was touching what was mine...what became mine the minute she gave herself to me the night before. "You sure you're okay?"

What the fuck was going on? I got the distinct impression that I had just missed something important.

She gave him a weak smile and removed his hands from her shoulders.

Well at least that made me feel a *little* better.

"I'm okay, I promise. I'll talk to you later."

"Okay. Just remember, I'm around if you need me."

"Thank you."

He turned and headed for the door, but not before shooting me a death glare. I gave as good as I got, hoping he'd spontaneously combust as he walked through the door, closing it behind him.

When I turned back to look at Taylor she had her hip cocked—which was never a good thing to see on a woman—and her arms crossed over her chest. I wasn't too proud to admit that the icy look she shot me had my balls shriveling up just a bit.

"What are you doing here, Jordan?"

"I needed to see you," I answered pathetically.

She let out a humorless laugh. "You needed to see me? Wow, well you didn't seem to need to see me this morning when you were sneaking off without saying a word, did you?"

That was a question I *knew* I shouldn't answer.

I saw her eyes dart down to my hand that was holding the flowers. "And you thought bringing me flowers would make up for turning my first ever sexual experience into a one night stand?"

Whoa, was that what she thought? "Taylor that is *not* what happened last night."

"Oh, so you didn't act like a typical guy and use me as a quick fuck?" The sarcasm in her voice was really starting to become irritating.

"Christ, woman. No! Where, in everything that I said to you last night, did you get the impression that I just used you as a quick fuck? Huh? You know that's not true."

"Then where'd you go?" she yelled.

"I got paged to a goddamn crime scene!" I yelled back. I could see her guard falling the second the words left my mouth.

I came to see her because I needed a little brightness in my day and all I'd received was more darkness. It was turning out to be one of the worst days ever. "It was two in the morning and you were sleeping. I got a call that they found a body and I didn't want to wake you. You looked so peaceful. I just couldn't lay that shit on you. I'm sorry I left without telling you, but I didn't do it for the reasons you think. I tried to call you so many times today, I swear, but something always got in the way."

I dropped the flowers on the coffee table and turned for the door. "I'm sorry," she whispered as my hand hit the cold brass of the door knob causing me to pause before opening it. When I turned back to her she was messing with that damn locket again. "I'm sorry," she repeated before taking a step toward me. "I...when I woke up this morning and you were gone...I didn't even consider that it could have had something to do with your job."

I made my way back over to her and cupped her face in my hands. "Crimson, that's the *only* reason I'd ever leave a bed that you're in."

That blush I was coming to love crept up her neck and onto her cheeks. "Do you want to talk about it?"

I let out a groan and collapsed onto her couch, pulling her down with me. I laid my head on the arm before kicking off my shoes and propping my feet up on the other end. I maneuvered her little body so that it was lying on top of me with my arms wrapped around her delicate frame. When I finally had her in the position I wanted her in I let out a contented sigh.

"Comfy?" she asked with a laugh. She rested her palms on my chest, propping her chin on them so that she could look up at me with those beautiful copper eyes.

"I am now," I said with a smile, making sure my dimples stood out. It wasn't lost on me that Taylor melted a little every time she saw them, and sure enough, they had the desired effect when all of the rigidity left her body and she relaxed completely in my arms. "Now we can talk."

"Tell me what happened."

I thought back to the woman whose body we'd found early that morning and a sense of helplessness washed over me. She'd gone through more pain than the other victims had, which was another sign that the killer was escalating. Not only had he kept her for a shorter amount of time, but his attack was much more brutal than it had been with the others.

"Her name was Samantha Turner. She was young and beautiful and had so much life ahead of her."

I heard Taylor's gasp and something passed over her eyes but disappeared before I could name it. "You're the detective on the Poet murders?"

"Yeah," I muttered as I let her go to press the heels of my palms into my forehead in an attempt to offset the headache I knew was coming. "Four girls and we're no closer to finding this guy than we were in the beginning. Days like this, I really hate my job."

My eyes were squeezed shut so I missed the apprehensive look on her face, but then she trailed her fingers down my cheek and I knew I could have gotten lost in her touch forever.

"You look exhausted," she whispered.

"I *am* exhausted." I replied, still not opening my eyes.

I felt her body shift. I finally peeled my eyes open to see her sit up and straddle my lap. All of the sudden I wasn't feeling so tired anymore.

"Tell you what, I've got that big, cozy bed back there that's just calling my name. If you promise not to run out of here in the middle of the night without telling me, I might be inclined to let you join me."

I pushed up onto my elbows and quirked a brow. "Is that so?"

"Yep," she replied playfully. I'd never seen her playful side before, but when the full force of that smile hit me it became my favorite of all her looks.

"That's a promise I'll have no problem keeping, Crimson."

///

The Poet

I despised night clubs. The heavy thump of the bass, the women who dressed like sluts and writhed on the men for attention, the disgusting smell of sweat and sin that stifled the air. There was nothing I liked about night clubs.

But shortly after Samantha had let me down, I was walking down the street, absorbed in my misery at having another woman disappoint me when a beautiful angel stumbled into my path as if she'd fallen from heaven. I was instantly enamored.

"I'm so sorry," she said as she looked up at me. The moment our eyes connected I knew there was something special about her.

She wasn't like the others.

"No worries," I replied. "Are you all right?"

She smiled up at me and my heart melted. "Yeah. I'm just running a little late and tripped trying to rush inside."

She pointed to the entrance of a nightclub I had just walked past and a twinge of disappointment shot through me at the thought of an angel working in such a despicable establishment.

"You should come inside and let me buy you a drink, handsome," she offered, and with that, I knew she was the one for me.

I'd followed her for a while, getting a feel for her schedule and I made sure to visit her at the nightclub every time she worked, even though I despised it.

Relationships were based on compromise, after all.

But there was something different about her tonight. She didn't look as happy to see me as she usually did.

When I made my way to the bar she didn't greet me with the lovely endearment that was just for me.

"Hey there, what can I get you?"

I felt my dormant anger simmering at the fact she would talk to me like I was just any other patron. Didn't she know who I was to her? Didn't she know that we were meant to be together?

I tried to push away my negative thoughts and give her the benefit of the doubt.

"I'd be honored if you'd allow me to take you on a date tomorrow night."

She turned her head to the side but not fast enough to hide the roll of her eyes. "Sorry, I'm spoken for," she declared.

Lying bitch!

In all the times I watched her I'd never seen her with another man. I couldn't let my disappointment crush me. There wasn't time for that. She was another filthy whore that needed to pay for her sins.

And it was my job to make sure she did.

Taylor

Something woke me in the middle of the night but it wasn't a nightmare. I opened my eyes and scanned the darkness around me trying to get my sleep-muddled brain to kick into gear. I felt something move behind me and I instantly became aware of what woke me.

"I know you're awake," Jordan whispered before pressing his lips to the sensitive spot between my ear and shoulder and nipping at the skin lightly.

I let out a sleepy moan when his hand trailed across my stomach, brushing along the bare skin between my shirt and shorts. "Mmm, I love the sounds you make when I touch you."

His hand skimmed passed the waistband of my shorts and into my panties. He pushed a finger inside me and started thrusting quickly. There was desperation in him that wasn't there the last time we made love.

"That feels so good." I turned my head as far as I could and his lips met mine in a passionate kiss. He quickly added another finger and I had to wrench my mouth free from his on a gasp. "Oh, God, don't stop," I cried as my hips started chasing after his hand every time he pulled out.

"I want you to come for me, baby. I'm going to make you come on my hand right now, then again when I'm buried deep inside you."

"Yes," I hissed.

My hips bucked harder when he began to circle my clit with his thumb while his fingers did amazing things inside me. "You want me, Taylor?" he asked and I felt like I'd go insane if

I didn't have him. I nodded frantically as my climax built up but that wasn't enough for him. "Say it, baby. I need to hear you say it."

"Oh God, Jordan. I want you!" I was so close. I could feel my release creeping up and I was desperate for it.

"Tell me you need me," he rasped in my ear.

I knew I'd tell him anything he wanted to hear at that point. I'd beg him if he asked me to. "I need you…please."

He slammed his mouth down on mine and curled the two fingers inside me in a come hither motion as he pressed down hard on my sensitive clit. I went over the edge gasping and moaning uncontrollably.

"Jesus Christ!" He quickly shifted me to my back, and before I could register what was happening, he'd ripped my shorts and panties down my legs and whipped my shirt over my head. He reached for a condom on the bedside table and quickly rolled it on. He rested his hips between my thighs and I instinctively wrapped both of my legs around him. "Do you have any fucking clue how sexy you are when you come, Crimson? I'm never going to get enough of you." With that, he thrust his hips and buried himself as far as he could go. I let out a loud cry at the overwhelming pleasure as he started to move. All of the pain I'd felt the last time was gone and the only thing on my mind was how absolutely perfect Jordan felt inside me.

For such a sweet man, I was surprised at the level of intensity he was taking me with. It wasn't making love like some people would describe. It felt like more. It was a claiming…he was marking me as his with each powerful thrust and I loved every second of it. Another orgasm was building fast and I wanted so badly for Jordan to send me over the edge again but he had different plans.

"Not yet, baby."

I looked at him with wide eyes. "What?"

"*Fuck*," he hissed. "I can feel you squeezing the shit out of me but you can't come yet."

I clenched even tighter around him at his demand. "I'm so close. Oh God! Please, Jordan."

"Not. Yet." His teeth were clenched and I could see his jaw ticking at his effort to maintain control. He grabbed hold of both my hands and lifted them above my head, twining our finger together as he looked down at me with a fierce determination in his gorgeous hazel eyes. "You're mine. You know that, right?"

"Yes. Jordan...please."

"You have no clue how perfect you are," he whispered. I felt tears sting the back of my eyes at the sincerity in his voice. He released one of my hands and wrapped his arm around my waist, pulling my body even closer to his and lifting my hips to the absolute perfect angle. "Let go, baby. I want to hear you."

I came shouting his name until my voice went hoarse. I didn't think it was humanly possible for anything to feel that good but Jordan just about killed me. Once I finally started coming back down, I was able feel how close he was. His thrusts were more erratic and his hold on me tightened to the point where I thought I might find bruises the next morning. "Holy shit. God, Taylor, you feel so fucking good. Nothing's ever been this good." He threw his head back with a bellow as he drove into me one last time before he stopped moving all together, keeping me pinned to him as tightly as possible the entire time he came.

After several long seconds, he eased his hold on me, slid his arm out from behind me and used it to brush the hair out of my face. Affection lit up the features of his face and I found myself lifting up to kiss him. He kissed me back for several seconds before pulling back just a fraction and running his nose along the side of mine.

Then he said something so touching any chance of protecting my heart disappeared entirely. "All day long, all I kept thinking was how badly I wanted to get back to you. All the bad things I saw, all the darkness, none of it matters when you're around. All you have to do is smile and I'm able to forget the bad and remember how beautiful the world can actual be. You give me that."

I ran my fingers through his unruly blond hair and looked him in the eyes, hoping he could see the importance of what I was about to say. "You give me normal. No one has ever given me that."

He kissed me again before replying, "I'm quickly realizing that I'd give you just about anything if it made you happy."

His body left mine, and before there was a chance of being affected by the cold, Jordan pulled the comforter up and tucked it around me then went to the bathroom to take care of the condom. I was almost asleep when I felt the bed dip as he climbed in. His arm hooked around my waist and he pulled my back flush against his chest then let out a contented sign. "Never get enough, Crimson." He whispered into my hair before sleep took over both of us.

///

Two weeks. For two weeks things between me and Jordan had been fantastic. I hadn't had any more visions or nightmares in that time and I was blissfully happy. I should have known it wasn't possible for the good things in my life to last.

"Are you sure there isn't anything I can help with?" I asked as I sat at the breakfast bar in Jordan's kitchen watching him make dinner. We usually stayed at my place but he had called earlier that day to ask if I could come over so he could cook for me. I wasn't about to pass up a free meal. I just hoped he knew what he was doing in the kitchen.

"Nope," he said as he strained the pasta over the sink before turning back to the stove top. "Just sit there and look sexy."

I glanced down at my outfit, a Benny's Diner t-shirt, blue jean shorts and my running shoes. I wasn't exactly dressed to the nines. Add to the fact I didn't have any makeup on and my hair was in a sloppy ponytail and I was really starting to second guess Jordan's judgment.

"Stop looking at yourself and thinking I'm crazy," he said without even turning around to face me. In the past couple of weeks he'd become even more in tune with me than he was before. It was almost scary how well he could read me.

"Get out of my head, freak."

He turned and gave me a wink. "Stop making it so damn easy to read you."

"Whatever," I grumbled. "So what are you making me anyway? And is it going to give me food poisoning?"

He turned and threw a piece of chopped carrot from the salad at my head. "It's angel hair pasta with chicken Pomodoro. And I'll have you know that I'm an excellent cook."

"Ahh, did I offend that delicate male pride of yours?"

He dropped the spoon he was holding on the countertop and started for me. Just before I was able to jump off the stool and make a run for it, his arms banded around me, effectively pinning my own arms to my sides as he began to tickle my ribs.

"Stop! Ah, Jordan!" I squealed as I laughed uncontrollably.

"Say I'm the best cook in the whole world," he demanded.

"You're the best, I swear! I didn't mean it!"

He finally stopped tickling me, but I was still laughing and out of breath when he moved his hands from my hip up to cup my cheeks. "So beautiful," he muttered more to himself than to me. I turned my face into his palm and planted a kiss in the center of it before looking back into his hazel eyes. I didn't think I'd ever get enough of looking into them.

I opened my mouth to tell him how special he made me feel but a sharp, splitting pain rushed through my skull knocking me off balance. Jordan caught me before I hit the floor but my purse hadn't faired so well. I'd knocked it over and the contents scattered all over his floor.

"Christ. Taylor, are you all right?"

Not now. Please not now. I chanted in my head over and over. I didn't want Jordan to witness me having one of my visions but I wasn't going to avoid it and risk not seeing the victim I was supposed to help.

I squeezed my head in my palms, trying to control the stabbing pain pulsing through it as I stood up. "Excuse me," I groaned as I stumbled to the bathroom and locked myself in.

"Taylor!" Jordan pounded on the bathroom door trying to get in. "Baby, are you okay? Let me in."

"Just a second," I called weakly. The last thing I needed was for him to bust the door down. "It's just a migraine. I'll be out in a minute, I promise."

All I could do was hope that I'd placated him for as long as it took to see if I could make out who was in the vision. The pounding on the door stopped so I lowered the toilet seat, dropped down and closed my eyes. I inhaled and exhaled slowly as I attempted to calm my mind and open up for the vision to become clearer.

Dark hair flooded my sight as the woman's image started to form more clearly. She was on the ground, struggling with someone. I could feel the terror coursing through her veins as if it was my own, but unlike the other visions there was something other than terror the woman was feeling. It was almost like…determination. She kicked her leg as hard as she could and connected with her attacker's body, causing him to release her long enough to let her go. I still couldn't make out her face but I watched as she climbed to her feet and ran blindly in the hope of finding a door. The door she found looked like it was made of heavy steel, and I felt as she struggled to push against its weight. There was a set of bare wooden stairs right outside the door, but before she was able to start climbing, her attacker grabbed her hair and spun her around.

Oh God. No!

I watched as Cassie's face came into perfect focus, right before her attacker raised his arm and plunged a knife into her chest.

Romance, who loves to nod and sing,
With drowsy head and folded wing,
Among the green leaves as they shake
Far down within some shadowy lake,
To me a painted paroquet
Hath been —a most familiar bird—
Taught me my alphabet to say—
To lisp my very earliest word
While in the wild wood I did lie,
A child—with a most knowing eye.

Of late, eternal Condor years
So shake the very Heaven on high
With tumult as they thunder by,
I have no time for idle cares
Though gazing on the unquiet sky.
And when an hour with calmer wings
Its down upon my spirit flings—
That little time with Lyre and rhyme
To while away—forbidden things!
My heart would feel to be a crime
Unless it trembled with the strings.

"Nooo!" I screamed at the top of my lungs. Not her. Not Cassie. Seconds later, the bathroom door came crashing open, sending splintered wood flying across the floor. Jordan stood there with wide eyes, panting heavily as I began to cry uncontrollably. I jumped off the toilet and flung myself at him in desperation. I needed his help. He was the only one that could possibly help me stop Cassie from being killed.

I wrapped my arms around his neck and tried to calm myself enough to talk as he lifted me into his arms and carried me into the living room. "Jesus, Taylor. You're scaring the fucking shit out of me. What the hell is going on?"

He sat on the couch, still not letting me go as he turned me to straddle his lap and took my face in his hands. "What's happening? Please, talk to me."

My heart was beating at such a fast tempo because of what I'd just seen and what I was about to do. Odds were, Jordan was going to think I was certifiable after I told him the truth, but I had no choice. He was my only chance.

"I'm going to tell you something and I need you to listen before you talk, okay?"

He looked leery but nodded anyway. I reached for my locket and squeezed it so tightly it cut my palm, drawing blood but I couldn't let it go. "When I turned seven I started to have these…visions. I saw one of my classmates being abducted and murdered, but when I tried to tell my teacher, she accused me of lying just to get attention. I went to the principal and even tried telling my parents, but they all blew me off saying I was being irrational. I tried to confront the girl and tell her what was going to happen but she thought I was crazy and told her parents that I threatened her. They came up to the school to talk to the principal and it became this huge thing."

I paused to suck in a breath before pushing forward. "The principal and my teacher told my parents that maybe I needed psychiatric help, so they found the most expensive doctor they could and forced me to go see him. They didn't give a shit about me really; they just wanted people to think they were getting their poor daughter the help she needed."

"What happened to the little girl?" Jordan asked in a hushed voice.

I dropped my head, not able to make eye contact as I told him. "A month after I had the vision she was kidnapped while she was playing in her front yard. They found her body three days later."

I felt Jordan's whole body stiffen beneath me and when I finally looked up I couldn't make out the expression on his face, but deep in my gut, I knew nothing good was going to come from telling him the truth.

"Why are you telling me this now?" he finally asked after a silence that lasted way too long.

I pushed past the knot in my throat to tell him the rest of it. "I've been having visions and dreams of women being murdered but they haven't been clear. A few weeks ago I had a vision of a blonde woman being chased by someone. It was Samantha Turner."

Jordan took his hands off me and ran them through his hair. His demeanor had changed in such a way that I felt the need to put a bit of distance between us. I slid off his lap toward the end of the couch and he did nothing to stop me. "Taylor, it was probably just some sort of nightmare. You must have seen something on the news about Samantha Turner having gone missing and it probably just manifested itself into a dream."

The desperation was building back up again and the terror I recalled feeling from each of the women as they struggled against their attacker was so intense I felt as if I would choke on it. "No, Jordan. That's not what happened. I saw her. I saw her being chased then I dreamt about how she died."

"That doesn't mean anything…"

I cut him off the only way I knew how. The poems left on the women's bodies were never released to the public so there was no way of knowing what the poem was.

"I am not yours, not lost in you," I started. "Not lost, although I long to be. Lost as a candle lit at noon, lost as a snowflake in the sea…"

I let my voice trail off when his eyes grew huge and he jumped from the couch. "How do you know that poem, Taylor?"

"It came to me in my dream about Samantha," I whispered. "I told you I saw how she died. She was stabbed to death." It wasn't a question. I already knew the answer. I just needed him to realize what I was saying was true. "She had a cut on her cheek that went all the way to the bone and another the length of her stomach."

Jordan became erratic as he crouched down in front of me. "How the fuck do you know all of this, Taylor? Who told you?"

"No one told me!" I yelled. "I saw it. She was bound to a mattress in a pitch black room. He toyed with her before he killed her." I started to cry again as I recounted the gruesome details of that dream. I needed him to believe me. "He tortured her and terrified her. He forces all of the women to tell him that they love him before he kills them!"

"ENOUGH!" Jordan bellowed. He grabbed hold of his hair and pulled in frustration while sucking in deep breaths. "Taylor," he started, the distress evident in his voice. "I need you to tell me who gave you all this information. None of this was released to the public. If someone's leaking information that is supposed to be confidential it could seriously jeopardize this case."

"I already told you how I know! I've seen these murders. You have to believe me, Jordan," I pleaded. "I saw Sylvia Garcia being strangled to death. I saw Samantha Turner being stabbed. I saw him tell each of them that he'd let them go if they just said that they loved him. I felt their fear as they said the words and when he screamed that he didn't believe them right before he took their lives!"

He was pacing the living room frantically, mumbling incoherently. "Jordan," I cried. "His next victim is Cassie. I know the poem he's going to leave folded up in her hand."

"No," he shook his head violently.

"Yes, Jordan." I began reciting the lines from memory. "Romance, who loves to nod and sing, with drowsy head and folded wing. Among the green leaves as they shake far down within some shadowy lake…"

"Stop! Just stop," he demanded. "How could you possibly know that?"

My shoulders drooped and my head fell into my hands. He wasn't going to believe me. He wasn't going to help. I didn't hear him fall to his knees in front of me so I was startled when he reached for my face and held it so aggressively I flinched in pain. "Do you know him?" His voice caused my skin to break out in goose bumps. "Do you know who the killer is, Taylor?" he asked as he gave my head a shake.

"No," I wept.

"I can't help you if you don't talk to me. If you're involved in this I need to know. You can trust me. I'll do everything in my power to help you." He went from frantic to sad. The expression on his face was one of heartbreak. He truly believed that I was somehow involved in the murders. It was easier to think that I was capable of something so horrible that it was to believe that it came to me in a vision.

I didn't even register my hand going up in the air and coming down on Jordan's cheek until the loud crack echoed through the room. There was no mistaking my handprint as the red indentation on his face started to form. "How dare you!" I screamed. "How could you possibly think I'm involved?" It was my turn to pace his living room. "I was with you the night of Samantha's murder. We were together from the moment you picked me up until you got the call. You *know* I wasn't involved! I told you exactly how I know all of this. I'm not making this up, I swear."

He rose to his feet and stomped off in the direction of the kitchen. When he returned he was holding something in his hands that I couldn't see clearly until he thrust it at me. "Then explain these," he said in a tone so cold it actually caused me to cower. What he had just shoved at me almost slipped out of my fingers, but when I was finally able to get a good grip on it,

I turned the burnt orange medicine bottle in my hand and read the label.

"Where did you get this?" I asked on a whisper.

"They fell out of your purse when you knocked it over on the bar. You expect me to believe that you have visions of people dying when you're taking Thorazine? You're on a goddamn antipsychotic, Taylor!"

"I KNOW!" I yelled at the top of my lungs. "You think you need to remind me that I've been taking drugs my whole fucking life to suppress the images I see? I'm more than aware of that Jordan! But I'm telling you now, I'm not involved in these murders and I'm not fucking crazy. Cassie is next and I'm not going to stand here fighting with you when I should be out trying to help my friend."

I ran into the kitchen for my purse then started for the door. I'd just cracked it open when he came up behind me and slammed it shut, effectively trapping me between him and the door.

"Where are you going?"

"To help my friend since you won't do it," I replied as I tried to push him back.

"Taylor…" he started, but I cut him off. I spun around and looked in those hazel eyes that I'd begun to fall in love with. The same eyes that made me believe that I could live a normal life just like everyone else. The light that I'd seen behind them was gone and the only thing reflecting back was doubt and concern. Doubt that what I was saying was true. Concern that I was insane. It was the same look I'd been getting from people my entire life and seeing it on Jordan's face just about killed me.

"We're done," I stated with as much finality as I could muster. "Whatever this was between us is finished. You made me believe that you were someone special. Someone who would have my back when everyone else in my life abandoned me the minute I needed them. You're just like everyone else, Jordan." With a final shove, I pushed him a few steps back from the door, yanked it open and did what I was always forced to do.

I ran.

The Past

"Mr. and Mrs. Taylor, I'm sure you understand how serious the stories your daughter is telling are. We just can't tolerate her going around telling other children that they're going to die."

My father nodded solemnly at the principal, Mr. Whitaker, as he spoke.

"Of course we understand, Mr. Whitaker, and I can assure you that we'll be taking immediate action to rectify the situation. We've already scheduled Lydia to meet with a doctor to help understand why she insists on lying," my mother replied, putting on her best concerned parent face.

At seven years old I'd already figured out that there wasn't a single maternal bone in her body, and that her demeanor was all an act for the outsiders. She was gifted at making people think that she and my father actually gave a damn about me, when in all honesty, they'd have been happier if I'd never been born at all.

"Thank you so much for your prompt attention, Mrs. Taylor. I'm confident that you'll be able to get Lydia in line."

I knew arguing with them would get me nowhere so I just sat in the corner with my head lowered and my hands clasped so tightly in my lap that my knuckles were turning white.

"I promise you we will. Thank you, Mr. Whitaker." With that, both of my parents stood and headed for the door. I followed behind them obediently, knowing that my punishment for embarrassing my mother would be even worse if I didn't.

"I can't believe you did this to me and your father, Lydia," my mother hissed under her breath as we pushed through the doors of my elementary school and made our way through the parking lot. "What kind of sick, twisted little shit makes up stories about their classmates being murdered?"

"I didn't make it up," I mumbled through the knot forming in my throat as I tried to keep the tears at bay. Crying just made her even angrier.

My mother spun on her heels and slapped me across my face, sending a flash of fire through my cheek. If I'd learned anything in my life, it was that I should never show any type of reaction to my mother's physical abuse.

"Yes, you did!" she yelled once we were far enough away not to draw any attention. "And I don't want to hear another word about it. We're going to see Dr. Lansing first thing tomorrow. You're just as crazy as Marilyn." My mother always sounded disgusted at the mention of my grandmother's name. I used to wonder how a person could possibly hate their own mother as much as mine did, but as the years progressed and I got older I was quickly coming to understand.

"What did I ever do to deserve having to put up with the two of you?" I could have listed so many examples but I was smart enough to know I needed to keep my mouth shut. "I won't tolerate you embarrassing me the way she did." She spun around to face me in the back seat, looking at the locket around my neck with disgust. "You're never going to see that woman again," she said coldly. "I'll not have her putting these insane ideas in your head."

My mother was a woman of her word. I never saw my grandmother again. She was the only person who could have helped me understand what was going on in my mind, but she was gone. My mother cut off all contact and she died shortly after my twelfth birthday. The only reason my parents had a funeral for her was to keep up appearances. I spent the day of the funeral locked in my bedroom, mourning my loss by myself since I wasn't allowed to attend. When people asked why I wasn't there, my mother tearfully responded that it was because I was taking my grandmother's death hard and she didn't want to put me through any more pain.

I was truly alone.

I was forced to see Dr. Lansing once a week until I left home and moved to Seattle. Nothing about those sessions helped me in any way. He agreed with my mother and was convinced that I told lies to get attention.

Then two months after my first vision, Jodi Harrington was abducted from her front yard by someone in a dark blue van. A few days later she turned up dead. It took weeks before the police found any leads into who could have kidnapped and murdered her. And once the truth came to light our picture perfect suburb was rocked to its core.

Apparently Jodi's uncle suffered from a mental illness and was sicker than anyone in his family was willing to believe. He was convinced that he was saving her soul from eternal damnation because she had been born with the devil inside of her. During questioning he confessed to killing her in order to save her.

He never made it to trial. He had been in a psych hospital during trial preparation and the hospital staff found him dead in his room a week before the trial was supposed to start. He'd hung himself.

My mother and Dr. Lansing were convinced that I didn't have visions. They were hallucinations caused by schizophrenia and that what I saw and what happened to Jodi were merely coincidental. I was immediately put on antipsychotic medication.

People at my school couldn't understand how I knew about what was going to happen to Jodi. Some were convinced that I was in some way involved, but seeing as I was only seven that was just ridiculous. Others jumped to the conclusion that I was insane. Once word spread about my medication I became an outcast. None of the children had anything to do with me unless it involved making fun of or harassing me, and the teachers just kept their distance, throwing nervous looks my

direction whenever I walked by. The panic attacks only led me
to becoming even more of a pariah than I already was.

The visions never stopped, but as time went on, I realized
that the medications helped to suppress them somewhat, so I
stayed on them, never wanting the full effect of seeing the
things that had already ruined my life.

///.

I ran out of Jordan's apartment building like I was on fire.
As soon as I cleared the doors I pulled my cell phone from my
purse and frantically started dialing Cassie's number.

Voicemail.

I hung up without leaving a message and called Benny's.
When she answered I asked if Cassie was there but when she
told me no I hung up without saying another word and pulled
up the web browser, quickly looking for the number for Dark.
The person who answered informed me she wasn't on the
schedule for that night so I hung up and tried her cell again.

Nothing.

I was starting to lose it…heart beating a staccato rhythm.
She was in danger and I couldn't reach her. She wasn't at either
of her jobs so I did the only other thing I could think of. I
jumped in my car and headed for her house. I didn't know
where else to go.

It was the longest car ride of my life but when I finally
pulled up in front of her row house I threw my car in park and
jumped out, making a mad dash for her door. I pounded on
the door like a mad woman, yelling her name as tears blurred
my vision and rushed down my face.

I'd just about given up hope when the front door swung
open and a sleepy, yet worried looking Cassie stood before me.
I launched myself at her and wrapped my arms around her
neck as my panicked crying changed into relieved sobs.

"What the hell, Taylor? Is someone dead?"

I couldn't hide the visible cringe at her words. "You weren't...answering your...ph...phone," I managed choked out between breaths.

"Hey, hey. It's okay," she soothed as she pulled me into her house. "It's all right, Taylor. I'm here. Everything's going to be okay."

She pulled me over to the couch and sat with her arm around my shoulders as I continued to cry. "You're really starting to scare me, Taylor. What happened? Are you hurt?"

I tried my hardest to get a grip and calm myself down. When I finally thought I would be able to talk without having another meltdown I looked at Cassie and did my best to explain. "I don't know how to say this to you without sounding completely insane."

"Just tell me, hon. It's okay." Her support gave me the strength to say what I needed to say.

Her kindness was overwhelming. I wanted to lay it all out for her but I knew I couldn't risk it. If there was a chance she'd disregard what I told her because she thought I'd lost my mind I would never be able to live with myself.

"You're in danger," I finally blurted out, causing her eyes to widen and her spine to stiffen. "I can't explain how I know this because it wouldn't make any sense, but I need you to trust me," I finished knowing that was asking a lot.

"There's someone out there that wants to hurt you and I think it may be someone you met at Dark. I haven't seen anyone at the diner that gives me the creeps so that's the only other place I can think of where he'd see you."

"You think someone's stalking me?" I could tell she was starting to get scared by what I'd just admitted. "Who?"

I shook my head weakly. "I don't know. I know you probably have a million questions and I wish I could answer them, but I just can't. I don't have any of the answers myself. All I know is that someone wants to hurt you and I think you should take a vacation from Dark for awhile. Maybe you could go and visit family out of town or something? I'm so sorry, Cassie. I know I sound like a lunatic right now and you probably want to get as far away from me as possible but I need you to believe me," I pleaded.

She stared for several seconds, just watching me cry before giving me a slight nod. "Okay," she finally replied.

I was stunned. "Okay? You mean you believe me? Just like that?"

She sighed and leaned back against the arm of the couch, pulling her knees to her chest. "I don't know what to believe, honestly. No one wants to hear that they're in danger but I've never seen you so freaked out in all the time I've known you. If you're this upset then you obviously have good reason and I'd be stupid not to listen to you. So…yeah, just like that."

The tears broke free again and I went in for another hug. I knew I was squeezing her hard but I'd never felt so much relief in my life. "Too tight," she wheezed. "Can't breathe."

I released her and mirrored her posture on the other end of the couch. "So you're going to take a break from Dark?" I asked needing to hear her say the words.

Cassie gave a slight shrug before replying, "Yeah, why not. I'm exhausted anyway."

I gave a small laugh and repeated the words she'd told me. "A girl's gotta do what a girl's gotta do for Jimmy Choo."

She threw her head back and let out a loud laugh. "This is true but I think I've got enough pairs to last me a while." All of a sudden her smile disappeared and was replaced with a serious expression. "I don't think you're insane, Taylor," she said with so much conviction it warmed me inside. "I think you're smart and funny and loyal, and I'm proud to call you my friend."

"I'm proud to call you my friend too," I whispered.

I come to and lift my head to look at my surroundings but all I see is black… dark, overwhelming black. I'm trying to recall what happened but my brain is sluggish and I'm having difficulty remembering. My shoulders ache but when I go to move them I can't. My breathing picks up

and I try to kick my legs but nothing happens. I try to shift and the feel of hard wood presses into my back.

I'm on a chair. Or more to the point, I'm tied to a chair, but with what I don't know. When I move my wrist to try and feel what's securing me in place, nothing's there.

That can't be right.

If there's no rope or tape, why can't I move? My struggles stop when I hear the sound of a heavy door being pushed open somewhere behind me. My heart rate picks up and I find it difficult to breathe.

All I can think is that I don't want to die here, in this dark, dank room.

Something hard and cold is pressing against the bare skin at the back of my neck and I shiver noticeably at the feel of it. Whoever is standing behind me continues to run it along my shoulder and down my arm. When the tip of it presses into my skin harder I realize it's a knife.

I try and move away from it but the effort is in vain. A deep chuckle sounds in my ear and I can smell the cologne of whoever is standing behind me. It's familiar but I can't place it.

"You're so beautiful," the deep, gravelly voice tells me.

Where do I know that voice from? I'm certain I've heard it before.

"You're not like the others," he continues, making a chill of terror and disgust rush up my spine. "You're strong, so much stronger than all the women before you. I thought they were meant for me but I was wrong. It was you. All this time, I've been waiting for you."

He makes a move with the knife and it feels like my invisible bonds are cut, freeing me to move my arms. He makes his way in front of me but I still can't see his face in the darkness. He releases each ankle and pulls me to standing. I'm flush against his body and it takes all of my willpower to keep the bile from rising in my throat at his intimate caress.

"You're so different. So brave…so determined. We're soul mates," he whispers as he runs his nose along the line of my jaw. I can't hold back the tremor that courses through me or the whimper that escapes my throat. I've never felt so full of terror and hate.

"Tell me you love me," he says as he licks the shell of my ear. Tears start falling down my face and I can't hold back the sob that breaks through. "Shh," he soothes. "Tell me you love me and I'll let you go."

I know he's lying. He's never going to let me go. If I don't fight I'm going to die here. I feel his hand reach up into my hair. Pain rips through my scalp as he wraps his hand around a large chunk of my hair and pulls roughly. "I said tell me you love me and I'll let you go," he hisses.

I won't do it. I'm not going to let my last words on earth be a lie simply to placate this psychopath.

"No," I say through clenched teeth. Before I can register movement, I'm sprawled across the damp concrete floor, the taste of copper in my mouth from my split lip and a throbbing in my cheek. I have to get out of here. Now is my only chance. I'm not bound to the chair or being held on to so I need to make a run for it.

I push up and start for where I heard him enter minutes earlier, but he grabs hold of my arm before I can make it. I spin around and frantically swing my fist through the air. I can't see where he is so all I can do is pray I hit my mark. From the sound of crunching bone and his loosened hold I know I have.

My arm is released but before I can take a step he reaches for my ankle and pulls me to the ground. I let out a scream as I crash to the floor with a painful thud, feeling the painful snap of my ribs as some of them break.

But I'm not giving up.

I kick my foot out and connect with what I can only hope is his face. He yells out in pain as I push up, ignoring the stabbing agony in my side as I run for the door again.

I'm at a wall, running my hands along the rough cinderblocks, looking for a latch…a knob…anything to get me out of this god forsaken room.

My hands sweep across cool steel and I know I've found the door. Adrenalin is coursing through my veins at the realization that escape is so close. I grab hold of the latch and push the door open. It's much heavier than I anticipated and it takes a lot of effort.

It cracks open and I can see light spilling down what looks like bare, wooden steps. I'm in a basement of some sort but where, I don't know.

I take a step out of the room but before I can make it to the stairs he grabs me by my hair and spins me around. "You stupid bitch!" he yells. "You're just like the rest of them! You're nothing but a filthy fucking whore!"

The light coming down the stairs illuminates his face and I instantly recognize him. My mind screams just as the knife in his hand plunges down.

I woke up like I always did after a nightmare like that, drenched in sweat and gasping for breath. It was Cassie in that nightmare and it me living through it. I didn't see her face, but there was no doubt in my mind that it was my friend.

I glanced at the clock and saw the numbers glowing 6:45 in the morning. I knew she'd be pissed but it was a chance I was willing to take. Ever since leaving her house three nights ago, I called and texted regularly just to make sure she was okay. She always answered.

The phone rang in my ear just before her muffled, sleep filled voice broke through the line. "Still alive, hon," she said. "But you won't be if you don't cut the early morning wakeup calls."

I let out a little laugh and heard her giggle in return. "Sorry, go back to sleep."

I pulled the phone away from her ear when her voice came through again, causing me to bring it back up so I could hear her. "Hey, Taylor?"

"Yeah, Cass?"

"Love you, friend."

Tears burned the back of my eyes as I replied, "Love you, too."

Jordan

I'd been blowing Taylor's phone up for the past three days to no avail. After she ran out of my apartment I went into the liquor cabinet, cracked open a bottle of bourbon and began working my way through it. When I started the bottle I was replaying everything Taylor told me about seeing visions of people before they died. It was just too ridiculous to believe.

A quarter of the way through the bottle I started questioning how she had the information she did on the murders. There wasn't a single cell in my body that thought she was involved in any way. Unfortunately, my rational mind wouldn't let me consider the fact that what was she was saying could possibly have any truth to it.

Halfway through the bottle I started questioning my decision to automatically believe what she was saying was either a lie or just plain crazy. And I wanted to kick my own ass for how poorly I had handled the situation with her meds. I'd been the world's biggest asshole. She was right. I'd let her believe I was in her corner and that I'd always be there to support her and the minute the words left her mouth, I knew I'd treated her the exact same way everyone else in her life had. I was worse than her parents. At least they'd never given her false hope.

I didn't remember much after that but when I woke up the next morning I remembered the look on her face as she told me what had scared her so badly. I remembered the look of fear that quickly changed into disappointment at my reaction before turning into total devastation when I accused her of being involved then threw her pills at her.

The pain that my guilt caused was the only thing that overshadowed the pain from my hangover. I'd been falling for that girl more and more with every day that passed and I'd broken her trust that I'd all but begged her for.

I needed to talk to her more than I needed air.

"Dude, when are you going to get the fuck over that little waitress? You've been moping around here for the past three days. Even I'm starting to get depressed and I'm a naturally jovial person," Stevens said as he leaned back in his desk chair causing it to let out a groan that told me it was dangerously close to the end of its life.

"Stevens, you don't even know what the fuck the word jovial means so just shut your goddamn mouth."

"She dump your whiny ass because she realized you have a vagina?"

He just didn't know when to quit.

I got up and started walking away before I broke my partner's face…not that anyone in the department would really blame me. Barry Stevens was a great guy, but he had a mad talent for pissing people off in only a matter of seconds.

"Where you going?" he called after me as I pulled my keys out of the pocket of my slacks.

"Lunch," I replied right before pushing through the precinct door. I hopped in my car and drove to the place where I knew I could find Taylor.

Unbeknownst to her, I'd been keeping track of her schedule for the past few days. I never went into her apartment building or Benny's Diner but I was keeping a constant eye on her. Yeah, I knew I was quickly reaching stalker level but that girl had me tied in knots.

I couldn't function.

I would watch her from a distance and the one thing that stood out most was that as I watched her she watched Cassie. When they worked together, Taylor's eyes would constantly dart over to wherever Cassie was. It was as if she had to see her to make sure she was still okay. That just intensified the guilt for not taking what she said seriously. It was obvious she believed what she'd told me and it didn't take a genius to see that it was weighing heavily on her.

I don't know how long I sat in my car outside of the diner, but I was so engrossed in my "stalking" I hadn't even noticed someone watching me. I really wasn't showing my skills as a detective.

The knock on my window scared the ever living shit out of me and I about spilled my coffee in my lap when I jumped.

The last person I wanted to see was standing there wearing a smart-ass smirk on his face while I tried to recover from my near heart attack.

"What the hell do you want?" I asked the smug looking bastard after I rolled down my window.

"I'd ask the same thing," Daniel replied. "But since I've seen you in this same spot for the past three days I think I've pretty much got it figured out." He turned his head toward Benny's right as Taylor walked past the big plate glass window.

"Why don't you mind your own fucking business," I pouted like a ten year old. Jesus, maybe Stevens was on to something. I *did* sound like I was growing a vagina.

"Taylor is my business, ass face."

Good to know we both sound like whiny ass kids.

"Oh? And how do you figure that? I thought you said you were never involved."

Daniel let out a sigh and then proceeded to open my car door. I braced myself for a fight but it never came. "Come on, copper," he said as he stepped back on the curb. "You and I have some things we need to discuss."

I hesitantly got out of my car, closed the door and engaged the locks. "Where are we going?"

"There's a coffee shop a few blocks up. I've got some stuff I need to tell you and I need you to listen with an open mind."

I looked up at the sky and let out a groan. "Why does everyone keep saying that? It's becoming a fucking trend."

"Quit your belly aching and let's go."

We walked in silence for a few minutes as we headed for the coffee shop. Once there, I pulled the door open and was instantly hit by the welcoming scent of freshly brewed coffee. I'd already had four cups that day but was in desperate need of more. Since Taylor walked out of my apartment I hadn't gotten more than an hour of sleep each night...not counting the night I passed out from my bourbon bender.

We placed our order and remained quiet while we waited at the counter. Once the barista called our names, we made our way over to a booth near the back where it was somewhat secluded.

"All right," I started skeptically once we were both seated. "What is it you have to tell me?"

He ran a hand over the back of his neck and frown lines indented his forehead. Whatever he had to say wasn't going to be good. "I know what Taylor told you," he said in a hushed voice. "And I know you didn't believe her."

I opened my mouth to speak but he lifted a hand to stop me. "I'm not saying I blame you for doubting her but you have to know that what she told you...it's all true, Jordan. There are things in this world that are beyond anyone's comprehension. Just because you've never experienced something yourself, doesn't mean it's not true. Taylor's had this gift since she was seven and it's been my job all this time to watch over her."

I was having trouble wrapping my brain around what he was telling me. "Like an instructor or something?" I asked lamely.

"You could say that. But think more along the lines of a guide. She had a shit childhood and I blame myself for not helping her when she needed it the most, but it was beyond my control."

I could tell he wanted to say more, but for some reason, he wasn't able to so everything he said came out rather cryptic.

"I don't understand. If you were both kids how were you supposed to help her with the things that were going on?"

"That's a question I can't answer even if I wanted to. The answer is so far outside your realm of reality there's no way in hell you'd believe me. Not yet anyway."

I was growing more and more aggravated at his evasiveness. "Why don't you try me?"

He picked up his coffee and took a long drink. "No can do, buddy boy. We aren't here to talk about me. We're here to talk about Taylor. I'm sure by now you've seen the locket she always wears?"

My head shot back at his question. It was freaky how intuitive Daniel was. "Yeah. How can you miss it? Every time she gets uncomfortable she messes with the damn thing."

He leaned in like he was about to say something life altering. "That locket was her grandmother's. She gave it to Taylor on her seventh birthday because she knew what Taylor was."

I felt my brows shoot up to my hairline at his words. "Taylor's grandmother had the same gift she does and she knew that once Taylor turned seven the visions would start. She tried to prepare her for what was about to happen but Taylor's mom was a raging bitch who thought her own mother was loony so she wouldn't allow them to see each other. Marilyn was the only person who knew what Taylor was about to start going through, yet her own daughter prevented her from giving Taylor the help she needed."

I ran my hands through my hair and left out an exasperated breath. "Jesus Christ."

"There are other things in her past that I can't tell you, but I will give you this. Her real name isn't Taylor Carmichael, its Lydia Taylor. She had it changed legally the minute she turned eighteen and got the fuck out of that hellhole. You look into Lydia Taylor and you may get some of the answers you need."

He started to stand and anxiety began churning in my stomach. "Wait a minute. You can't just dump shit like this on me then bail out. None of this makes any sense!"

He pulled his wallet out of his back pocket and threw a couple bills on the table. "I've told you everything I can, Jordan. Just take the name I gave you and look into it."

"How do you know all of this?" I asked frantically. I needed more answers.

"I can't tell you that either." He started to walk away but paused just outside the door. I watched as he turned around to say something else. "It's not just a coincidence that you two were drawn together from the moment you met. There's a reason for everything and you two didn't just find each other by accident."

With that little bombshell, he turned and walked through the door of the coffee shop, leaving me more confused than before.

One thing was for certain though. I was sure as shit going to look into Lydia Taylor.

//

The rest of my day was a complete wash. If I wasn't thinking about Taylor, I was thinking about everything Daniel laid on me earlier. I ran a check on Lydia Taylor but wasn't able to come up with much. There were articles about a girl named Jodi Harrington being abducted outside of her home and a few of them mentioned Lydia spreading rumors about the kidnapping months before it ever occurred, but seeing as they were both minors at the time, all of the official information was sealed. It looked like Lydia had been under the care of a Dr. Lansing since she was seven but I wasn't able to obtain any of those files.

I was able to find one thing that might have been helpful though. In the records, there was a phone number for Charles and Julia Taylor. I'd written the number down before I left the precinct for the night, but once I got home all I could do was sit at my kitchen table and stare at the numbers I'd scrawled across the pieces of paper. Was I really going to call up these people and dig into Taylor's past for information? It felt like such a skeezy thing to do but I didn't see where I had much choice.

Daniel insisted that he was looking out for Taylor and he'd practically handed me this phone number on a silver platter. I glanced up at the clock and noticed that I'd been staring at the number for more than two hours.

No time like the present, I thought as I picked up my phone and began dialing the Connecticut area code. The phone rang three times before a woman with a heavy accent answered. "Taylor residence." She sounded Hispanic so at first I thought I'd misdialed.

"Uh...yeah. Um..." I stumbled through my awkward greeting before pulling myself together. "I'm looking for Mr. or Mrs. Taylor," I stated, trying my best to sound authoritative.

"Hold please," she said sounding bored.

I sat there for several minutes listening to people hustling around on the other end of the line before someone finally picked the phone back up.

"This is Julia Taylor," a harsh, disinterested voice said through the phone. I could only imagine how Taylor felt growing up with this woman as a mother. She'd only spoken four words and it was already evident that she was a total ice queen.

"Um, yes, Mrs. Taylor. My name is Jordan Donovan. I'm with the Seattle police department." I was eager to get as much information from this woman as I could so I introduced myself as an officer thinking it might soften her towards me somewhat. I was wrong. "I was hoping we could discuss your daughter, Lydia Taylor."

She made a sound that could only be described as a snort through the receiver before asking, "What kind of trouble has that girl caused now?"

I was thrown at her automatic assumption that Taylor had done something wrong. "I'm sorry if I gave you the impression that she's in some sort of trouble. That wasn't my intention, Mrs. Taylor."

"Officer Donovan, I don't assume Lydia is *in* trouble. I'm confident that she has *caused* trouble. That's all she has ever been good for."

My spine stiffened at the arctic chill blowing through the phone. "Mrs. Taylor, I'm not calling because she's done anything wrong. I'm strictly calling as a friend. I had a few questions and I was hoping you'd be able to shed some light on Taylor…I mean Lydia for me. I'm concerned about her."

Julia Taylor scoffed on the other end and I knew that calling her was a mistake. It was evident in her inflection that she wasn't going to lift a finger in an attempt to help her only child. "Officer Donovan, you sound like a smart man. The only advice I can offer you about my daughter is to stay away from her. She's a one woman wrecking crew. All she's ever done in her life is cause destruction. She made up ludicrous stories as a child strictly for attention and almost destroyed her father's political career."

"Are you talking about Jodi Harrington?"

Mrs. Taylor remained silent for several seconds. "I see you've done your homework. I'm sorry but I don't like to speak about that incident." She said with such finality that I knew I'd hit the nail on the head. "Lydia humiliated me and her father with her insane ramblings," she continued. "Do you have any idea how embarrassing it is to not only have one, but two mentally ill people in your family?"

"But she isn't mentally ill," I protested. How a person could be so cold as to refer to their own flesh and blood as an embarrassment was beyond me. "I've gotten to know her pretty well. I don't think there's anything wrong with Taylor's mental health." I didn't realize how strongly I believed that to be true until I actually spoke the words.

"So she goes by Taylor now? How clever," she offered with a cruel laugh. "Don't let the pretty little package fool you, Officer Donovan. *Taylor* is nothing but trouble. And if I'm being honest, not worth the time and effort you seem to be putting into her."

"Wow, when she said you were a cold hearted bitch I really thought she was exaggerating but after spending thirty seconds on the phone with you I can believe it. I'm sure there's a special place in hell just for you. Have a good evening." With that, I hung up.

I wasn't going to get anything useful from that evil bitch, and it took a lot more self control than I was willing to give to listen to her spew her bullshit about Taylor.

My determination strengthened after talking to Taylor's mother. I was going to prove that I wasn't anything like those people. I was going to show Taylor that she could count on me no matter what…and I figured I knew just the way to do that.

I picked up my phone and dialed the number by heart. "This is Officer Donovan. I need a car on a Cassandra Sinclair."

Taylor

"Are you ever planning on talking to him or are you just going to keep staring out the window every damn day?" Daniel asked as he looked over the menu with a bored expression.

I reached over and slapped him in the back of the head with my order pad. "Mind your own business or no more discounted meals for you."

"You're going to have to talk to him eventually, Taylor. He's been sitting in his car during his lunch hour all damn week, staring in here like a sad little puppy. I'd almost feel bad for the guy if he wasn't such a fuckwad."

I looked out the window at Jordan sitting in his black Sequoia. "He's probably watching me to make sure I'm not out killing anyone." I muttered as I sat Daniel's plate down in front of him.

"You don't honestly believe he suspects you, do you?"

I let out a sigh and turned away from the window of the diner. "He practically said so himself. Right before he threw my crazy pills at me."

"Taylor…" Daniel reached for my hand but I pulled out of his grasp. "He doesn't think you're involved."

I looked around uncomfortably, hoping no one had overheard our conversation before sitting in the chair closest to him and leaning in. "Daniel, I know things that haven't been released to the public, Jordan said so himself. What's the point of me having all these details if all it's going to do is make me a suspect? How am I possibly going to help anyone if I'm in prison?"

Daniel ran a hand through his jet black hair before finally making eye contact. "Taylor, don't you understand? If you didn't have the kind of information you do, there's no way anyone would have taken you seriously."

"But Jordan didn't take me seriously," I interrupted. "At best, he thinks I'm a nut job, at worst, a murderer."

He reached over and took my hands in his. "It was the only way, sweetheart. You have to know these things in order to stop this guy. If not, he's going to keep killing. You're the only person that has the capability of stopping him."

"No pressure there!" I scoffed.

When Daniel didn't have a comeback to my smartass remark I continued. "I'm scared," I finally whispered. "What if I can't stop him? What happens if I fail and Cassie dies because your higher power gave this gift to the wrong person?"

"I have faith in you. I know you can do this, Taylor. You just need to have faith in yourself."

With how my life had been, my faith in anything had been shaken at a very young age. I had no other choice but to pray Daniel was right. I'd already lost so much because of this so-called gift, Jordan included. I couldn't lose Cassie too.

I worked the rest of my shift speaking to as few people as possible. Each time I looked out the window and saw Jordan's car I felt an irrational sense of anger. Anger at him for being another person in my life who let me down, but mostly anger at myself for missing him as much as I did. The vicious cycle continued when I'd glance over and see his car gone. The anger would disappear and be replaced with sorrow at the loss. I couldn't understand why I still cared about him as much as I did after how heartbroken I'd been at his reaction when I confided in him.

"Evening, Gary," I said as I walked past his desk and to the elevator banks.

"Evening, sweetie. You look upset, everything okay?"

I gave him a sad smile and kept walking as I called over my shoulder, "I'm just tired. It was a long shift."

I saw the concern on his face but I was too exhausted, physically and emotionally, to try and pacify Gary.

As I unlocked the door of my apartment, my cell phone started going off in my purse. I looked at the display and a sense of dread crept down my spine.

"Cassie? Is everything okay?"

"Everything's fine, worry wart," she replied with a laugh. "I was just wondering if you had any clue why I've been followed around by cops for days."

"Huh?"

"Yeah. They've been on my ass like white on rice. If it's not a patrol officer, it's your ex-boyfriend Douchey McAssface."

"I…I haven't got a clue."

Was it possible that Jordan had taken me seriously? I didn't think that was possible but I couldn't come up with any other explanation.

"Well, I don't know what he thinks he's doing, but that asshole is lucky I haven't walked up and kicked his balls up into his stomach for how he treated you."

After several days of watching me mope around, Cassie finally cornered me and made me tell her what was going on. I didn't go into detail about the vision I had of her but I did admit to her what Jordan had said when I reached out for his help. Needless to say, he was her least favorite person. And I loved her even more for her solidarity.

"Honestly, Cass…I don't have a clue why cops are tailing you. Did you hold up a liquor store or something?"

"Hmm," she mumbled through the phone. "Maybe they're on to that balloon of cocaine I have shoved up my—"

"Goodnight, Cass! I'll talk to you in the morning." I shouted before she could finish her statement. That was a mental image I did not need.

"Night, doll. I'll be waiting for my butt crack of dawn wake up call."

We hung up and I dragged my tired body to the bathroom for a much needed shower.

As I stood under the water letting it wash away all the grit and grime from hours at the diner, I also felt like I was washing away some of the tension I'd been carrying around. I felt a sense of relief knowing that there was someone watching over Cassie when I couldn't be there to do it. I didn't know if it was Jordan who'd been the one to set it up but I was grateful to whoever did it and for whatever the reason behind it was.

I don't know how long I stood under the steady stream of water, letting it beat down on my knotted muscles in my shoulders, taking the tension away with it as it ran over my body and down the drain but by the time I was finished I was more relaxed than I'd been in days.

Standing in front of my mirror, I did something I don't think I'd ever done before. I studied the image in front of me, truly getting a sense for the woman I wanted to be, the woman I was struggling to become.

Staring back at me wasn't a scared girl who spent every second hiding from life; it was a new woman, a stronger, more resilient woman. The shadows hiding behind my eyes were slowly starting to creep away and they shined more than ever before. I liked the Taylor I was becoming more than I'd ever liked the Lydia I used to be.

I was smiling at my reflection while I pulled a brush through my long, damp tendrils when someone started knocking on my front door. I pulled my robe from the hook on the bathroom door and slid my arms into it, then cinched it tightly as I headed toward the door.

Looking through the peephole and seeing Jordan standing on the other side caused millions of butterflies to start rioting in my belly. It wasn't fair that he still looked so gorgeous. No matter how hard I wished the feelings away, he still affected me like no one else.

I thunked my forehead against the door and breathed deeply. I didn't even have time to sort out my inner turmoil because he knocked again, but this time he also called out,

"Come on Taylor, open the door. I know you're in there. I just heard you."

"Damn it."

"Heard that too."

I yanked the door open and crossed my arms over my chest trying to appear annoyed when all I really wanted to do was launch myself in his arms and kiss the breath right out of him.

His blond hair was a little more disheveled than usual and he looked like he hadn't shaved in at least two days. The light stubble covering his cheeks and chin only made him look that much better. It wasn't fair.

I tried my best to not let my desire for him show but it was so difficult, especially when the longing in his hazel eyes shined through so clearly.

"Hey, Crimson."

My knees went weak at the endearment that I'd missed so much but luckily, I was propped against the door frame so he wasn't able to tell.

I kept my expression as blank as possible when I asked, "What do you want, Jordan? You here to arrest me? Or maybe you just want to hurl more accusations my way."

He reached up to touch my face but pulled his hand back when I flinched. "Please don't be like that," he said softly.

"Be like what?" I asked sarcastically. "I'm sorry, am I acting crazy again? Maybe I should have the doctor up my meds…"

Before I could finish my sentence he slammed his mouth down on mine. It wasn't a slow, sensual kiss. This kiss was full of yearning and before I could register what was happening I found myself melting into him. It took Jordan wrapping his arms around my waist and pulling me flush to his chest to snap me out of my lust filled haze.

I put my palms to his chest and pushed him as hard as I could. He only stepped back a few inches but it was enough for me to get out of his grip and suck some much needed air into my lungs. He'd managed to fry all my circuits with that one kiss.

"Don't," I said, holding up both hands as he came toward me again. He stopped hesitantly and I didn't miss the look of pain that shifted across his face at my rebuff.

"Taylor, I can't even begin to tell you how sorry I am for how I treated you." He took a step toward me, which brought him into my apartment. For every step forward he took, I took two steps back. "I'd give anything to go back and do that all over again," he continued.

"But you can't," I interrupted. "You can't go back and fix it. I've had enough people in my life who have treated me like a freak to know that a person's initial reaction is normally the most honest one. You proved exactly what you thought of me when you shoved that pill bottle in my face."

Jordan dropped his head and ran both hands through his hair roughly making it look even more chaotic. "I'm sorry," he said as he shook his head back and forth. "I'm so damn sorry, Taylor. You have no clue. I've been trying to sort out everything you told me from the moment you walked out that door. But you have to believe me...I never thought you were involved. I never should have said those things and I'll regret them for the rest of my life."

I didn't respond but I also didn't move when he came forward again. As much as I wanted to push him away and hate him for hurting me, I just couldn't. The pain etched into every line of his beautiful face ripped at my heart. He ran a hand over my cheek and gently brushed a strand of hair behind my ear before tangling his fingers near the nape of my neck. "I just didn't know what to think, baby. You freaked out, locked yourself in the bathroom and wouldn't let me in. I was losing my mind worrying about you. When you finally came out you starting saying things I'd never heard before and I just...I saw the pills and I reacted badly. I'm so sorry, Crimson."

I leaned my head into his palm as if it were second nature. His touch had a soothing quality that I needed so badly.

"As soon as you walked out on me I knew I'd just fucked up the best thing that ever happened to me. That's why I've been outside the diner every damn day. Not being able to touch you gutted me. There was no way I could get through a day without seeing your beautiful face."

Tears stung the backs of my eyes and I couldn't speak past the lump in my throat. I never expected to feel so strongly about a man in my life, especially a man that I'd known for such a short time.

"When Daniel came to talk to me and explained everything you'd been trying to tell me, I felt…well, I guess it made sense. And when I called your mother…"

"Wait…" My head snapped up, breaking the connection we'd just had. His words were like a bucket of ice water being dumped over my head. I pulled away like he'd burned me. "You called my mom?" His hand came back up but I slapped it away. "You had no right to do that!" I shouted. "How the hell did you even find them?" Then the realization hit me like a Mac truck. "You investigated me?"

There were things from my past that I'd never wanted him to see. Even though certain records were confidential since I'd been a minor, I never wanted him to know I'd seen a therapist at seven years old for psychotic behavior and delusions. All of that was a part of my past I'd been trying so desperately to escape.

"Please don't do that, baby," he pleaded. "Don't pull away from me. It kills me not to touch you."

I stalked over to the front door and yanked it open. "Well you better find a way to get used to it because you're never going to touch me again." He tried to grab my arms frantically but I fought against his hold. "Get out."

"Taylor…"

"Just get out!"

Tears started streaming down my face and I kept my eyes trained on the floor. I couldn't look at him. If I did, I'd cave. I couldn't cave. He had just ripped my heart out. I wouldn't allow myself to cave.

I felt him move to stand in front of me but I fought the instinct to lift my head. "I love you, Taylor," he whispered in agony before he turned and headed out the door.

He'd made it to the elevators when something dawned on me.

"Jordan," I called out.

When he turned back he looked almost hopeful.

"Did you put police on Cassie?"

The hope disappeared from his face when he realized I wasn't going to ask him to come back. He didn't speak, just gave a slight nod as an answer.

I reached up and brushed the tears from my eyes and attempted to give him a small, appreciative smile. "Thank you. That means a lot."

With that, I stepped back into my apartment and shut the door, collapsing against it as sobs wracked my body. Because the truth was, even though he'd hurt me worse than anyone ever had, I loved him too.

Jordan

Seeing the hurt in Taylor's eyes was like having my heart ripped out of my chest. I hated seeing that look on her face, but what's more, I hated that I was the one that put it there. I was never going to forgive myself for breaking her heart, and in the process, my own as well. There was just something about her that had gotten inside me and burrowed down deep. I'd never be able to get that woman out of my system even if I wanted to…which I didn't.

I didn't want us to be over. I wanted to hold her and comfort her when she needed me, but I'd been a jackass and now she wouldn't even let me touch her. Standing inches apart from her and not being able to feel her skin against mine was like a death in itself. I had to get her back.

She might have been determined when she said she was done with me but what she didn't know was that I was just as determined. It was going to take a *lot* of work but I was going to get her back. I hadn't known her for very long, but I already knew I couldn't function without her.

Taylor

"Benny, have you talked to Cassie?" I asked, growing more panicked with every passing minute. I'd texted her as soon as I woke up but she didn't answer. Thinking she was probably still asleep, I gave her a while longer before calling. All I got was voicemail.

Panic was clawing at me as I waited for her to call me back. I tried not to lose it but the clock was ticking and every minute my phone didn't ring was another minute that the terror crept closer.

"No doll, I sure haven't, but she may still be in bed. You know how that girl likes her late nights."

Benny didn't know the reason for my worry and I didn't want to dump it all on her. "But isn't she scheduled to work today?"

Benny glanced at the clock then back to me. "It's only 9:00. She's not late for another thirty minutes."

I couldn't wait thirty minutes. I was pissed at myself that I'd waited this long already. Shooting Benny a tight smile, I headed back toward the office and pulled my cell phone from the front pocket of my apron. I dialed the only person I could think of that could help me.

//.

Jordan

"Taylor?" The picture I'd taken of her one evening when we were at her apartment popped up on my phone. She had been laughing at something and I remembered thinking that she was the most beautiful when her guard was down.

Seeing her calling filled me with hope. That was until she spoke and I heard the panic laced in her voice.

"Something's wrong," she replied frantically.

My whole body went on alert at her words. Sitting at his desk across from me, Stevens became instantly aware of the tension filling me. "What do you mean? What's wrong?"

"I can't get a hold of Cassie. She's not picking up her cell or returning my texts."

"Calm down, baby," I said soothingly. "Maybe her phone's just on silent."

"No. No, she wouldn't do that," Taylor insisted. "She knows she's in trouble. I didn't go into detail with her but she knows I saw something bad happen to her and she wouldn't put her phone on silent. I check in with her all the time. She'd been expecting to hear from me this morning."

"Okay, it's all right. Just wait a minute and I'll make a call. Can you do that?"

She let out a relieved sigh on the other end of the phone. "Yeah. I'll wait."

I sat my cell down and grabbed the desk phone to put in a call to the officer I had sitting on Cassie's house.

"Matthews."

"Hey, it's Donovan. You still at Sinclair's house?"

"Yeah man, been here all night, everything's been quiet. Nice girl through. She brought me out a cup of coffee around midnight, tasted like shit but it was a sweet gesture nonetheless."

"All right. Listen, I'm heading over now. Be there in fifteen."

I hung up with Matthews and put my cell back to my ear. "Taylor, my guy said everything's straight over at Cassie's house but I'm going to go check it out for myself. I'll call you as soon as I know something, okay?"

"Yeah. Okay. Thank you so much, Jordan."

"Don't thank me, baby. I'm sure everything's just fine. I'll talk to you in a few."

I slid my finger across the phone to disconnect and grabbed my keys off my desk. Stevens was on my tail. "That about Taylor's friend? The one with the stalker?"

I wasn't exactly proud of myself for making up a stalker in order to get cops on Cassie but it wasn't like I could just tell people 'Hey, my girlfriend has visions and saw her best friend being killed by The Poet'. I had to come up with something plausible so I went with a stalker. Thank Christ I didn't say that it was an ex-boyfriend or something. I could only imagine what kind of shit storm that would stir up if something did happen to her.

"Yeah," I replied. "She hasn't been answering any of her calls. Taylor's kind of freaking out right now."

"Matthews say everything was on the up and up?"

"Yep, but I'd still feel better if I saw for myself."

"I'm with ya man." We headed out of the station and to the car.

Fifteen minutes later, I pulled up behind Matthews' Accord and saw him leaning against the driver side door. "I went and knocked after you called." I could see on his face that he was as concerned as I was. "No answer. I didn't see anyone going in or out last night but there was no movement when I knocked a few minutes ago."

The three of us headed up the narrow sidewalk to Cassie's front porch. Taylor was right, something was definitely wrong. I could feel it. The hair on the back of my neck stood on end and adrenaline started coursing through my veins.

"Shit man, I got a bad feeling about this," Stevens said from behind me.

That made two of us.

"Seattle police," I called as I knocked heavily on the door. Nothing.

I banged harder on the door hoping that she was asleep, or maybe in the shower. Still…I got nothing.

I looked over my shoulder at Stevens whose hand was resting on the butt of the gun at his hip. My gaze shot to Matthews and he gave me a small nod. It was completely against protocol but we needed to get into that house. All three of us knew that.

I took a step back and rushed the door, shoving my right shoulder into it as hard as I could. It didn't budge.

After two more attempts, the aging wood around the doorframe finally gave way with a loud groan and the door flew open.

"Son of a bitch!" Matthews called from behind me once I'd righted myself.

We'd barely made it two steps across the threshold before we were met with complete chaos.

The house was a wreck. Furniture was overturned, glass was broken, pictures were knocked off the walls and from the mantle above the fireplace. There had been a struggle…a big one.

We made our way from the living room into the kitchen where the backdoor that led to the alley behind the row house sat open.

"Jesus Christ," Stevens muttered.

"I swear, Donovan. I never heard a damn thing. I was out front all night and never suspected a goddamn thing had gone down."

I turned to Matthews and saw the distress etched into the lines on his face. "It's not your fault. Go radio it in. We need to get moving on this. Christ knows how long she's been missing."

He nodded his head and started for the front of the house. "I'm on it."

Taylor

I'd been nervously pacing the length of the office in the back of Benny's Diner for an hour after my call to Jordan, while simultaneously blowing up his phone. Every call went straight to voicemail. Benny came back to check on me a few times, but when she'd been unsuccessful at calming me down she just went back out front.

I'd finally decided I couldn't wait any longer so I grabbed my purse and rushed toward the front door when it swung open and Jordan and his partner Barry Stevens walked through.

The stoic expression on both men's faces knocked the breath out from my lungs; it caused my steps to falter.

"Where is she?" I whispered, feeling the tears building up in my eyes.

Jordan stepped closer and reached for my arms, trying to pull me in the direction of the office. "Why don't we go talk in the back?"

I jerked my arm from his hold and stepped up to him so that we were practically chest to chest. "Where is she?" I demanded so loud that most of the diner turned to see what the commotion was.

I felt soft hands land on my shoulders and turned to see Benny standing behind me. "Come on, doll. Let's not do this out here."

I allowed her to turn me and lead me away from the customers' prying eyes. I could hear the sounds of Jordan and Stevens following behind us but my thoughts were too chaotic to concentrate on their words. This wasn't right. I'd embraced the visions and had done everything in my power to stop them from happening. This wasn't right!

I entered the office and turned to look at them. No one said anything for what felt like an eternity. I saw a look pass between Benny and Jordan before she placed a hand on Stevens' forearm to get his attention. "Why don't I get you some breakfast? It's on the house."

I watched numbly as the two of them walked out the door and closed it softly behind them. When I turned back to Jordan, he was wringing his hands in front of him and I could see the ticking in his jaw from how tightly he was clenching it.

"Where is she?" I asked again, barely recognizing my voice. The tears I was trying desperately to hold back made it difficult to talk and my words came out raspy and broken.

"We don't know," he whispered.

With those three words my knees gave out, and if Jordan hadn't been standing so close, I had no doubt I'd have ended up on the floor. He pulled me to his chest and wrapped his arms around me as he backed both of us up and lowered onto a chair. He pulled me into his lap and stroked my hair soothingly. "We'll find her, Taylor. I swear. Forensics is combing every fucking inch of that house. If he left anything behind…anything at all, we'll find it. I'll get Cassie back."

Before I could respond, the office door flew open and Daniel stood before us looking more disheveled than I'd ever seen him.

"Taylor —" was all he was able to get out before I cut him off.

"I did everything you said. I stopped ignoring the visions. I did everything I could to keep her safe," I insisted.

"I know," he said morosely. "You did all you could. It's just that…after you do your job it's out of your hands."

I shook my head in disbelief. I couldn't accept that.

I wouldn't.

I turned back to Jordan and started telling him everything I knew. "There are stairs," I started. "He keeps them in a dark room. I never got a look at it with any of the other visions except for the one with Cassie…" I stopped and squeezed my eyes shut as the memories of that horrible nightmare came spilling back. "I think it's a basement or something. The walls were concrete…or cinderblock. There are stairs outside the room but they looked unfinished, you know…like the carpet or something had been torn up. I think they led up to a house but I don't know where. And a door! There's a heavy metal door. It's industrial or something…I don't know."

Frustration poured through me when I couldn't think of something more helpful.

"It's okay, baby," Jordan said, as he took my hand and gave it a squeeze. "It's okay, just take a breath."

I did as he said and sucked in a deep breath. When I felt a little calmer I opened my eyes and gave Jordan what I felt was the most important pieces of information.

"She's going to fight."

He shook his head in confusion. "What do you mean?"

I felt a tear run down my cheek and brushed it away with the back of my hand. "I saw her fighting him, Jordan. In my vision. She fights for her life harder than any of them did. She's so strong but that's going to set him off. You don't have much time."

At that, I broke down in tears again at the realization that the odds were, I was too late...again.

I sat on my couch holding a cup of coffee in one hand as I fiddled with my locket with the other. Daniel and Jordan flittered around the apartment trying to act like they weren't watching me like a hawk. If I caught one more side long look or pitying smile, I was going lose my shit.

I took a sip of lukewarm coffee and caught Daniel smiling at me from where he and Jordan were standing in my kitchen. I'd had enough.

"That's it!" I yelled. I'd finally reached my breaking point. "I'm tired of you standing here hovering over me." I turned to Jordan and asked, "Why are you even here? You need to be out there trying to find Cassie!"

"Taylor, we're just worried about you," Daniel said trying to extinguish the situation before it got too volatile.

I sucked in a slow breath and blew it out through pursed lips. I didn't mean to snap at Jordan but I was having enough trouble relaxing as it was. Jordan and Daniel weren't helping the situation by worrying about me when there were more important things to worry about. "I'm sorry," I explained to Jordan. "I didn't mean to yell. I just...I just need you out there looking for Cassie, okay? I know you're doing everything you can. I'd just feel better if you were out there not in here trying to take care of me. I trust you and I know you can find her."

Jordan's eyes changed from concerned to warm when I spoke. He walked up to me and wrapped his hands in my hair. "Okay," he said softly. "I'll get out there and look for her." He rested his forehead against mine and whispered, "Thank you for trusting me." He placed a gentle kiss on my lips and smiled sweetly before backing away. "Keep an eye on her for me, will ya?" he asked Daniel as he headed for the door.

Daniel saluted Jordan. "You got it, chief."

Jordan shot Daniel the finger before heading out the door to search for Cassie.

All of the anger I'd been holding onto in an attempt to protect my heart from Jordan disappeared the instant Cassie went missing. It was impossible to think of anything but getting her back. Finding her was all that mattered. Jordan was there and he was doing everything in his power to make sure Cassie was found. Because of that, I couldn't hate him any longer.

Once Jordan was gone, Daniel sat next to me on the couch and the look of pity returned to his face. "You doing okay?"

With that, I was done. I stood from the couch and sat my cup on the coffee table in front of me. "My best friend's been kidnapped and there's a chance she could possibly die. And I knew it was going to happen and couldn't do shit to stop it. How do you think I'm doing, Daniel?"

I didn't even give him a chance to respond. I just turned on my heels and walked away.

Jordan

I'd never felt so impotent in my entire life. I should have done something sooner. I had no one to blame for Cassie's kidnapping but me. It was my own damn fault. If I would have just listened to Taylor…if I had only believed what she was saying from the very beginning, none of this ever would have happened. Looking for a house with unfinished stairs leading to the basement was harder than trying to find a needle in a haystack.

"Fuck!" I shouted as I ran an arm over my desk, scattering everything on the top of it onto the floor. "There's not a goddamn piece of evidence in that entire house. How the fuck is that possible? With that kind of struggle Forensics should have had a fucking field day. You'd think they would've at least turned up blood or hair or something. It's like he's a fucking ghost!"

Stevens ran a hand over his balding head. "I don't know man…I don't know."

I couldn't think straight. My brain had been going non-stop while I functioned on no sleep for God only knew how long. I'd been wracking my brain for hours trying to come up with something that would help us find Cassie but I was still at a total loss.

Stevens' phone rang but I was so lost in thought I didn't even register what he was saying.

"Jordan…Jordan, did you hear what I just said?"

I was pulled back to reality when Stevens' hand landed on my shoulder. "Sorry… what?"

The look on his face told me everything I needed to know.

"There's another body." He dropped his head and gave it a shake. "It was The Poet."

No…Oh Christ, no.

//.

Bright yellow tape blocked off a large section of the public park as police and crime scene analysts worked to collect as much evidence as possible.

Walking toward the body, I couldn't help but pray over and over that it wouldn't be her. "What do we have?" I asked one of the medical examiners, a short, balding man with pale skin and a paunch that would rival Stevens'.

I took in the white sheet that was lying on the ground. Seconds later the sheet was pulled back and all of my hopes were crushed.

"License says her name is Cassandra Sinclair," the M.E. answered.

"Fuck me," Stevens muttered next to me before turning and walking away. By the look of pure anguish on his face, I knew he was feeling the same thing I was…guilt and pure rage.

"Death was caused by multiple stab wounds to the chest and abdomen," the pale man continued, "but from the looks of things your girl here put up one hell of a fight."

I spun around to look the pale man in the eyes. "What makes you say that?"

He pointed down so I could take in what he was talking about. "See the bruising on her left arm here?" I looked down to where he was pointing and saw a bright purple bruise in the perfect shape of a hand. "If you take a look at the knuckles on her right hand you'll see bruising and even more scratching. From what I can gather, it looks like he grabbed her by this arm here, and when he did, she spun around and swung at him with all her strength."

Taylor's words echoed to me as the medical examiner spoke.

"This asshole really did a number on her before he finally killed her. On top of all of the bruising, there's three fractured ribs, a shattered cheekbone, and a gash along the back of her head. It looks like he jerked her hair so hard he ripped it out, along with some of the skin."

"*Fuck*," I hissed out as I ran my hands down my face. Seeing Cassie lying naked on the cold ground was bad enough. Having to hear, in vivid detail, everything she went through was making my earlier breakfast threaten to make another appearance.

"Jesus Christ," Stevens said. "So basically, you're telling us that she was tortured before he finally killed her?"

I didn't want to hear the answer to that.

The guy dropped his head and shook it sadly before finally looking back at us. "I hate to say it, but yeah. This girl went through hell before she died. From the looks of her wounds, I'd say death was probably a relief."

Taylor

"Will you get that?" I was in the middle of pouring my fourth cup of coffee when I heard a knock on the door. I hadn't slept at all the night before, and I was running strictly off caffeine, adrenaline and worry.

I lifted my head from stirring in creamer and saw Jordan standing at the threshold, eyes rimmed red and glassy, hands shoved deeply into the pockets of the slacks he'd been wearing the night before.

One look at his face and I knew. The cup falling from my hands and shattering on the floor didn't even register as darkness started closing in. "No! No, no, no, no!" I sobbed as my knees gave out from under me.

Jordan was there in an instant, scooping me from the floor and carrying me into the living room.

"*No*," I screamed at the top of my lungs as my body shook uncontrollably. "Not, Cassie. No. Jordan, please. Please," I begged. "Not Cassie."

I could feel his tears dampening the collar of my shirt from where he had his face buried in my neck. "I'm so sorry, baby," he cried. Having this grown man crying on my shoulder as I broke down made my tears fall even harder. He held me in his lap and rocked back and forth. "I'm sorry. I'm sorry. I'm sorry," he repeated over and over.

Not Cassie. Please, not Cassie.

Even as I prayed, I knew there was no point.

I couldn't speak. I couldn't breathe. All I could do was sit in Jordan's lap and let the paralyzing grief take me over.

She was my friend. She was one of the very few people I'd let get close to me. I loved her.

And now she was gone.

She was gone and it was all my fault.

Jordan

"She finally asleep?" Daniel asked as I walked out of Taylor's bedroom.

I nodded my head. I had to make her take two Tylenol PM to get her to relax and with the help of the medication, she finally cried herself to sleep. She'd been in hysterics from the moment I showed up at her apartment and there was nothing I could do or say to help her. Seeing the woman I loved break down over the loss of someone close and not being able to do anything was the worst feeling I'd ever experienced. It was a knife to the gut.

"Why'd this happen, Daniel?" I asked, trying to understand, trying to wrap my head around everything that was going on in my life. "She did everything she was supposed to. Why'd she have to lose Cassie?" Tears stung the back of my eyes as I remembered seeing the pure anguish on her face.

Daniel leaned forward and rested his elbows on his knees. "Just because a Seer does what they can to prevent the loss of a life doesn't mean the outcome is always going to be the one we want. We can only do so much. Human nature does the rest."

"A Seer? So that's what she's called?"

"Yeah."

"So what's that make you?"

"I'm what they refer to as a Guide," he responded.

"You keep saying *they*. Who's *they*?"

"*They* are whatever higher power you choose to believe in."

"Wow," I replied. "Could you be anymore vague?"

Daniel let out a little chuckled and leaned back into the couch. "You asked, I answered, my man. Sorry if my response doesn't satisfy you."

I sat there in silence for awhile, trying to absorb everything I'd learned over the past few weeks. I had so many questions and I didn't know if I'd ever get the proper answers for them.

Still, I took a shot. "So, was becoming a Guide kind of the same process for you as becoming a Seer was for Taylor? I know her gift, or whatever you call it, didn't start to develop until she turned seven. Were you around the same age when it all started for you?"

He gave my question some thought before answering. "Not quite. I'm not really like you and Taylor," he replied.

"In what sense?"

He scratched the back of his neck and I knew that whatever he was going to say would be just as vague as before. "Let's just say that I'm…omnipresent."

I shouldn't have been surprised after everything that had happened since meeting Taylor, but I was. "You aren't even really human, are you?"

That question earned me another chuckle. "Not in the typical sense, no."

With that, I decided playing twenty questions with Daniel was a wash. I'd just lived through one of the worst days in my existence and wasn't up for letting it last any longer. Daniel finally decided to take off, and since there was no way I was leaving Taylor alone, I stripped down to my boxer briefs and crawled into her bed. I pulled her back to my chest and wrapped myself around her as tightly as I could without disturbing her. I let sleep wash over me.

I woke with a start a while later and noticed Taylor wasn't in the bed with me. With the exception of the red numbers glowing from the alarm clock letting me know it was just past two in the morning, the room was shrouded in darkness.

I slid from the warmth of the bed and into my pants to look for Taylor. A sense of fear washed over me when I couldn't find her anywhere in the apartment. I didn't even bother throwing a shirt on. Instead, I just ran out of the apartment to the elevator to get down to the lobby. I came skidding to a halt on the marble floor of the lobby, unfazed by the fact I was barefoot and shirtless.

I scanned the lobby and I saw no sign of Taylor but Gary was sitting behind his desk. "Have you seen her?" I asked.

With every passing second, I was growing more and more panicked.

Gary heaved a heavy sigh and pointed toward a hall off to the left of the elevators. "She's in the gym, son. She does this when she can't sleep. She wakes up in the middle of the night and runs her ass off to try and clear her head. You might want to get to her quick. From how she looked when she headed down here, I don't think there's enough running in the world to clear the darkness in her right now." He gave his head a shake. "I'm worried about that girl. I've never seen her so broken down. I don't know if she's going to be able to come back from this one."

She was going to come back from this. I'd make sure of it. Even if it took me dragging her back kicking and screaming.

///

Taylor

The whir of the treadmill normally overpowered the endless strip of flashes bouncing around in my skull and helped to tune out the constant noise rattling around inside. I woke up an hour ago and knew there was no way I'd get back to sleep. So I untangled myself from Jordan and decided to go for a run. It was one of the few things that always helped.

Except, this time it wasn't helping. The only thing in my head was Cassie, playing in a constant loop, over and over, never ending. Overwhelming grief was slowly suffocating me. It was hard to breathe.

I couldn't clear my head. I barely heard the whir of the treadmill as my feet pounded against it. All I could do was replay everything Cassie had ever said to me. There was one thing that stood out more than anything else.

Love you, friend.
Love you, friend.
Love you, friend.

I had to hop onto the sides of the treadmill to keep from falling off. Tears clouded my vision and the sobbing started up again. I felt a strong arm wrap around my waist as another came around and hit the stop button.

"It's okay," Jordan whispered in my ear. "Shh, it's okay, baby."

"It's not okay. None of this is *fucking okay!*" Jordan dragged me over to a weight bench and pulled me into his lap as I continued to cry. "This is my fault. All of it…it's all my fault. If I had just tried harder, if I…"

He grabbed my chin between his finger and thumb and turned my face to his. "It's not your fault, Taylor," he demanded. "You did everything you could."

"But I didn't! Don't you see? If I hadn't spent my life avoiding these visions maybe I could have stopped this. Maybe I would have seen something that could have helped…"

"Stop! Just stop, baby. You can't take the blame for losing Cassie, sweetheart. You have as much control of that as you do over what you see in your visions."

I pulled from his grasp and started pacing in front of him. "Then what's the point of this, huh? What's the *fucking* point, Jordan? Why do I have this goddamn gift if I can't do anything to save the people I love?"

Those last few words came out broken as the tears clogged my throat. I went down on my knees in front of Jordan and clung to his shirt in desperation. "Help me forget," I begged. I pressed my lips to his hoping to illicit a reaction. "Please, Jordan. Just help me forget. Just for a little while. *Please.*"

Jordan's hands wrapped around my wrists and made me release my grip on him. "You don't want this. You're mourning, Taylor. This isn't what you want."

He didn't understand, this had nothing to do with what I wanted. What I wanted was for Cassie to still be alive. This was about what I *needed*. I shook my head manically. "I *need* this, Jordan. You're the only one that can help me forget. I *have* to forget."

I kissed him again, and after a few seconds he finally responded and kissed me back. I buried my fingers in his silky blond hair and pulled with more force than I'd ever used before as I tried to intensify the kiss.

When he pulled back I was afraid he was going to stop me. He stood from the bench and reached for my hand. "Come on," he said as he pulled me from the ground and out the doors of the gym. As soon as the elevator doors closed he slammed me against the wall and attacked my mouth in a brutal kiss. It was exactly what I wanted. I didn't need slow, passionate loving. I needed rough and reckless...hard. That's what was going to help me forget, even if it was only for a little while.

Putting a hand under the back of my thigh, Jordan pulled it up around his hip and I followed suit with the other one. As soon at the elevator dinged on my floor and the doors opened Jordan was moving. He carried me through the apartment and into the bedroom where he dropped me on the bed and pulled my running clothes off while I worked the button and zipper of his pants.

It was only a matter of seconds before we were both naked and Jordan was spreading my thighs to make room for his hips.

He buried himself all the way in one hard thrust. My back arched off the bed at the wonderful combination of pleasure and pain. "God, yes," I panted. "Just like that, Jordan. Fuck me hard. I need it just like this."

He pulled out until just the tip rested inside me. "I know, baby. I know," he said against my lips just before he slammed back in. I cried out at the wonderful things he was doing to my body as he kept up his punishing pace.

I felt my climax building faster than it ever had before and I welcomed it. I didn't care about prolonging things. I just needed release...needed to clear my mind.

"Faster, Jordan."

Our sweat slick bodies moved against each other as I planted my feet in the mattress and lifted my hips to meet each thrust. "You're almost there, baby, just let go."

At his words, I tumbled over the edge of release, screaming out as the most intense orgasm I'd ever experienced coursed through my body.

"You're so fucking beautiful, Taylor. So perfect." Moments later, Jordan joined me in his release. His head thrown back as his pleasure took over, he let out a loud groan. His hips were still pumping until he'd drained every last bit of himself into me before he finally collapsed on top of me. I welcomed his weight and wrapped my arms and legs around him, holding on tightly.

"God, I love you, Taylor," he murmured into my neck before finally lifting his head and staring straight into my eyes. "I love you so damn much, Crimson. You're my world."

Tears instantly welled up and slid from the corners of my eyes and into my hair.

"I'll do anything for you. I just need you to know that."

I couldn't speak. All I could do was nod as he poured his heart out to me. Once we'd both managed to calm our breathing, Jordan pulled himself out of my body and I instantly missed the intimate connection. But he didn't go far. He pulled the covers back up over both of us and wrapped me in those strong arms of his. I'd told him what I needed to get myself through the night and he'd given it to me, no questions asked.

Seconds later we were both asleep.

A week had passed since I sat in a hard, cold folding chair and watched them lower Cassie into the ground. My best friend. The only best friend I'd ever truly had.

Benny sat on my right, Jordan on my left with Daniel standing behind me. For all the people I had surrounding me…supporting me, all I can remember thinking was how alone I felt.

Jordan refused to tell me anything about Cassie's death. He insisted that having the details wasn't going to help…that I shouldn't remember her the way she died, but how she was when she was alive.

I knew by how he spoke, that what Cassie had gone through must have been awful so a part of me was grateful to Jordan for protecting me from that.

After several days of not leaving my apartment, lying in bed while Daniel and Jordan hovered, I finally decided that I couldn't take it any longer. The longer I stayed in that apartment the more I felt like the walls were closing in on me. The only time I felt at ease was at night, just before I fell asleep when Jordan wrapped himself around me in my bed, blanketing me with his warmth.

Neither he nor Daniel left my side since Cassie went missing. And although I appreciated their support, the two of them were driving me out of my mind.

"Are you sure you should be working right now?" Daniel asked again…for the hundredth time.

When I woke up that morning I decided that sitting around all day wasn't doing me any good. I told them both that I was returning to work and needless to say, neither of them thought it was the best idea. On top of being worried about how I was handling losing Cassie, they were both concerned with my wellbeing since The Poet was still out there.

I not so nicely informed them that their opinions didn't matter for shit and that I was going, whether they liked it or not. Apparently to them, that meant I was stuck with Daniel sitting in my section the whole damn shift, eating discounted meals and bugging the hell out of me whenever I passed his table. If he wasn't such a good tipper I might have kicked his ass out.

"You ask me that one more time and I swear to God, Daniel, I'm going to have the kitchen staff spit in your food for the rest of eternity."

He held his hands up in surrender at the thought of tainted food. "You got it, boss lady. I'll shut up now."

I shook my head and walked away to go wait on my other customers. I was pouring a cup of coffee when the man at the table asked, "Bad day?"

I glanced from the cup to the handsome, smiling face looking up at me. He looked to be in his mid to late thirties with nice brown eyes and a few days growth on his face. I might have appreciated the genuine smile he was giving me if I wasn't hurting. But even with all the bad things that had happened, Jordan was still at the forefront of my mind and I didn't have it in me to look at another man as long as Jordan was in my life. And he'd made it pretty clear over the past week that he wasn't going anywhere.

Even though he told me several times a day that he loved me, he never once made me feel pressured to say it in return. I knew my feelings for him hadn't changed but I just had too much coming at me from every direction. I had enough trouble just making it through the day. I didn't have it in me to stop and think about what my feelings for Jordan meant right then.

I returned his smile with one of my own, only difference was I couldn't make mine reach my eyes. "Yeah, you could say that."

"It's always a shame to see such a beautiful woman so unhappy."

I gave a small laugh. "You're very sweet for saying that."

"Well it's true. If there's anything I can do to put a real smile on that face, please let me know."

"Thank you…"

"Bryan," he offered as he held out his hand for me to shake.

I took his hand and shook it politely. "Thank you, Bryan. That's very kind of you."

"No problem," he looked at my name tag. "Taylor."

The rest of my day went about as same as the morning had. I walked through the day not really paying attention to much of anything, simply faking my way through it.

By the time I got home I was exhausted, both mentally and physically. All I wanted to do was soak in a nice, warm bath before crawling into bed and hopefully passing out.

As soon as I opened my front door I realized those plans were a bust.

"Seriously?" I asked as I looked at Jordan. He was in my kitchen, cooking dinner like he owned the place. My stomach let out a groan of hunger when the delicious smell of whatever he was cooking hit my senses, but I wasn't about to admit that to him. "I've had a bad day; an even shittier week and you just wrecked my plans for the evening of a bubble bath and bed. How did you even get in here?"

Jordan put the spoon he was using to stir some kind of sauce on the countertop and turned to me. He at least had the courtesy to look guilty. "Gary let me in. He and I both agree that you shouldn't be alone right now. We think you could use the company."

I threw my purse down on the bar separating the kitchen from the living area with a huff. "What I could use is some peace and quiet," I declared. "But it's pretty clear that you and Daniel…and apparently Gary…aren't going to give me that."

Jordan came around the island to where I was standing and lifted me up so I was sitting on the counter and we were at eye level. "Look, I know Daniel and I are driving you a little crazy…"

"Understatement. Of. The. Century," I interrupted.

He ran the tips of his fingers along the tops of my arms and goose bumps broke out over my skin. "Okay, so we're driving you a *lot* crazy," he conceded. "I know you're a private person and that we're stepping on your toes but it's almost over, I promise." He whispered the last few words and pressed his lips against mine. I got so lost in the kiss that I almost missed what he'd just said. I jerked myself back from him so I could see his face.

"Wait. What do you mean it's almost over? Did you find this guy?"

The thought of Cassie's killer being caught was like a jolt to my system. I hadn't realized until that moment how badly I wanted The Poet found. Unfortunately, street justice wasn't an option and since I wasn't what you could consider a vigilante, all I could do was hold out hope that something horrible happened to him in prison.

"We're looking into a potential lead," he said, still touching me. It seemed that if we were in the same room together Jordan always found a reason to touch me. His hands were somewhere on my body at all times. It was like he was afraid I'd disappear if he didn't feel my skin against his. It felt like an electric jolt whenever he touched me.

"What lead?" I asked, trying to sound unaffected by his closeness.

"Well, remember that door you told me about in your vision?"

I nodded my head as I recalled the last vision I had of Cassie.

"I got to thinking about it and I realized, the kind of door in your vision sounds like a commercial grade impact door. That's not something typically you see in a residential home and most of the time they have to be professionally installed. We're looking into who's had a door like that installed in their house in the last year."

My mouth dropped open and my eyes bugged out. "Holy shit! Jordan, that's fantastic!"

He hit me with that brilliant dimpled smile of his and a shiver shot up my spine. "It's all because of you, baby. We wouldn't have anywhere to go with this case if it weren't for you. You helped us."

My mouth went dry and I felt that familiar ache between my thighs that only Jordan could cause. "Why do you do that?" I asked quietly when his thumb brushed along my jaw line.

His eyes were on my lips when he asked, "Do what?"

"Touch me." At my answer, his gaze darted from my mouth to my eyes and the passion in the beautiful blue-green depths was so intense I couldn't look away. "You...you always find a reason to touch me." My breathing was growing erratic and I was sure he could hear how loud my heart was beating. "Like you're afraid I'm not real or something."

His lips tipped down at the same time his brows tilted inward. "Sometimes, I'm afraid you're not," he said. His voice so low I barely heard him. "I'm afraid if I close my eyes for just a second you'll be gone again. I know you don't trust me, but I wasn't lying when I told you it killed me not to touch you. It's like you've become an obsession for me. There isn't a moment that goes by in the day where I don't think about you. It's hard for me to even function if I don't at least get to see your face."

He leaned in and ran his nose from my ear to my collarbone, giving it a tiny nip that caused me to whimper. His words, his touch, his smell...everything about him made my blood run hot.

He pulled back and stared down at me. "I love you so much. It physically hurts to think I can't have you." He placed a hand at the center of his chest and rubbed like he was trying to soothe the pain away.

The sadness on his face broke my heart. All I could think was how much I wanted to make it go away. I didn't want to be the cause of his pain. I placed my hand on his cheek and he instantly pressed into it, turning slightly to lay a kiss on my palm. He squeezed his eyes shut like he was trying to memorize the feel of my hand on him so he didn't see the tear that ran down my cheek before I brushed it away.

"I love you too," I whispered. "I love you so much, Jordan."

I wasn't able to get another word out because the second I professed my feelings he was on me, hunger and passion bleeding from his lips to mine. He kissed me like I was air to him. I fed off his need for me; let his want fuel me as I pulled at the buttons on his shirt in an attempt to get to bare skin.

Jordan separated his lips from mine just long enough to rip the remaining buttons off his shirt and slide it down his shoulders to the floor before he was kissing me again. Placing his palm in the center of my chest, he pushed so that I was lying on the counter. My body was so feverish, the cold seeping into my skin from the marble didn't even register. The only thing I was thinking about was how badly I needed to feel him inside me and that he was taking way too damn long getting my shorts off.

"Please, Jordan," I whimpered.

My desperation must have echoed how he felt because my shorts were gone before I could blink and I heard the distinctive noise of his ripping my panties from my body.

"I'll buy you a new pair," he panted as he whipped his belt off and dropped it onto the growing pile of clothes.

"I don't care. I need you in-" Before I could finish my sentence Jordan had pushed his jeans past his hips and buried himself inside me in one thrust. "*Oh God!*"

"Look at me," he moaned as my back arched off the counter and my eyes clamped shut at the pleasure. "I need to see your eyes."

I did as he asked and looked directly at him as his hips moved at an almost punishing pace. "Say it," he demanded.

"I love you," I breathed just as my climax took over. I cried out his name at the same time I raked my nails down his naked back. It was too intense; I couldn't help it. My head flew back and my eyes drifted shut again of their own accord.

Jordan wrapped and arm around my back and pulled me up to sitting before taking my chin and tipping my head back down. "Again."

"I love you, Jordan."

"Christ, Crimson." He slipped his hands between our sweat slick bodies and started to circle my clit, applying the perfect amount of pressure.

I let out a strangled cry and tried to move his hand away as my release started to build back up again. "Jordan…it's too much. I can't…"

His forehead rested against mine as he kept the pace with his hips and fingers. "You can, baby. I've got you. This time your eyes stay on me."

He pressed down hard with his thumb and pulled out to tip before slamming back into me. That sent me over into a climax so strong I screamed my release. Miraculously, I managed to keep my eyes on him the entire time. "Say it again," he demanded as aftershocks rippled through my body.

"I love you," I said as tears streamed down my cheeks.

At those three words, Jordan came so hard I was afraid his knees would give out. His face was buried in my neck as he licked and nipped and sucked at the sensitive spot just above my collarbone, both of us breathing like we'd just run a marathon.

"Wow," was all I could say once I was finally able to form words.

I collapsed back onto the counter with Jordan resting his head between my breasts. I could feel his body shake against mine as he let out a chuckle. "Just wow? I guess I need to step up my game."

I shook my head and smiled down at him, loving the happiness shining in his eyes as opposed to the earlier pain. "I can't form any other words. I think you killed me."

Jordan turned his face to nuzzle the spot between my breasts and placed a soft kiss before looking back up at me. "I love you so much, Taylor. You're my world."

I felt my cheeks growing hot at his intensity. "I love you, too."

He crept up my body until we were face to face and his forearms were resting on the counter on either side of my head. "I'm pretty sure I fell in love with you the first time you blushed for me, Crimson."

I let out a laugh and wrapped my arms around his neck. "Well, it's good to know my embarrassment is attractive to you."

"Everything about you is attractive to me. And I plan on spending the rest of my life proving that to you."

The love I felt for him grew even more as he spoke about the rest of our lives.

Later that night, Jordan and I were lying in my bed with him sprawled on his back, one arm wrapped around me stroking my hair while I used his shoulder as a pillow. The room was dark with the exception of the lights from outside shining through the blinds. We'd been lying in silence for at least an hour and I was completely content. I was tracing the shadows on his bare chest when he finally spoke.

"What happened to make your day so bad?"

I lifted my head and gave him a confused look.

"When you got home you said you'd had a bad day."

Once I got over my initial shock a wide smile spread across my face. "You remembered me saying that?"

He smiled in return. "Don't sound so surprised. I remember everything you say, hell, I remember everything about you."

"Can you blame me for being shocked? We've had sex twice since then. I figured your brain would be worthless by now."

Both of his hands spanned my ribs and he dug his fingers in, tickling me as I thrashed around the bed laughing until tears were streaming down my face. "*Stop!*" I screamed while laughing hysterically. "Okay, okay. I take it back!"

He pinned me back to the bed and rested just enough of his weight on me so that I couldn't escape. "Tell me you love me and all's forgiven."

I smiled again and ran a hand through his tousled blond hair. "I love you, baby."

His fingers were laced together on my stomach with his chin resting on them. He was staring up at me with so much love in his eyes; it warmed me from the inside out. "Ooh, I think I like it even better when you add "baby" to the end of it."

"I'll have to remember that."

He reached up and grabbed my hand that was playing in his hair and brought it to his lips to kiss my knuckles. "So, you going to tell me what happened today?"

I sighed and thought back to everything that happened at the diner. "It wasn't any one thing in particular, it was just… hard…being there, you know, without Cassie." My voice cracked before I could stop it and I swallowed loudly past the lump in my throat.

"I'm so sorry, baby. I wish there was something I could do to make all this easier on you."

I sniffed and batted at the tears that had managed to escape. "You just being here helps me."

I didn't realize until the words came out, exactly how much I meant them. I'd already admitted that I loved him, but it was more than that. I trusted him. Even though he'd hurt me, he proved himself time and time again that I could put my faith back in him.

He must have sensed the real meaning behind my words because his face became soft and he lightly kissed my stomach. "It wasn't all bad," I continued. "Other than Daniel being a typical pain in my ass, the rest of my customers were pretty decent. I'm pretty sure one of them was hitting on me," I said with a little laugh.

Jordan's face grew tense and I felt his posture go rigid. "What's the fucker's name?" he asked between clenched teeth. His attitude made me laugh even harder.

"Oh, look at you all jealous. It's so cute."

He let out a snort and rolled his eyes. "It's not cute. It's rugged and manly."

I bit my bottom lip to try to hold in another laugh. "Okay."

"Seriously, give me his name. First and last... and a driver's license number would help if you got it."

It was my turn to roll my eyes. "Well, I don't have his license number but will a social help? We exchanged social security numbers when we decided to run off together and get married."

The tickling began again but he was more brutal than the first time and didn't stop until I about peed myself and gave him Bryan's name. "Not funny, Crimson. You aren't marrying anybody but me."

"Is that right?" I asked as I tried to catch my breath.

"Damn straight. I'm going to marry you and knock you up so you can't ever get away."

I scoffed at his sexist attitude and punched him in his shoulder. 'If you're looking for me to be the perfect little barefoot and pregnant wifey, you've got another thing coming."

He wrapped both arms around hugged me tightly. "I don't expect you to be anything but yourself. That's who I fell in love with, and that's who I want to spend the rest of my life with."

"I love you, baby."

The soft look crossed his face again and shortly after, we both fell asleep wrapped around each other.

The Poet

She was my angel of mercy. There was no doubt in my mind.

After having so many women lie to me and hide who they truly were, I'd finally found the one God intended for me.

I had seen her from time to time when I was watching Cassie, but I'd let my desires for that whore cloud my judgment and I'd almost let this beautiful creature slip through my fingers.

I knew she was mine from the moment our eyes met.

She had so much sorrow behind her beautiful amber colored eyes and I called to the pain behind my own. The both of us had experienced so much disappointment in our lives and I knew God created us to heal each other.

This woman was exceptional and it pained me to have to walk away from her.

Our time would come.

Like all great romances, we had to go through pain before we could come out on the other side and appreciate the love we had for one another.

I would be patient.

I couldn't risk losing her. All of the heartbreak I had experienced would be well worth it when I held my love in my arms.

It was only a matter of time.

Taylor

Two days had passed since I finally told Jordan I loved him, and my mood had been brighter ever since.

"Well good morning," a voice said to me.

When I looked over I saw Bryan sitting at a table in my section. "Good morning, Bryan. How are you doing?" I asked politely.

"I'm wonderful now that I've seen you."

My smile slipped slightly but I tried to maintain a cheerful demeanor. "Well that's nice of you to say." I wanted to turn the conversation away from anything potentially flirty so I asked, "What can I get you this morning?"

He lifted his menu and looked over it for a second before ordering. I quickly scribbled it down, offered a smile and bolted from his table, hoping I didn't look too obvious.

"What's wrong with you this morning?" Daniel asked. He'd come to the diner every day since Cassie died so he'd been privy to the change in my mood. I'd risked heckling and finally admitted to him that telling Jordan I loved him was what had put the smile on my face.

"Nothing," I insisted. "There's nothing wrong."

"Bullshit. You have that constipated look you get when you're all uncomfortable."

"Oh, that's a wonderful comparison. Thanks for that."

He waved his hand like he was blowing off my reaction. "You know what I mean. You look uncomfortable about something."

I fidgeted with my locket because he was right and I hated to admit that. "It's really not a big deal. It's just that I think one of my customers has a thing for me."

He looked around the diner trying to see who I was talking about. "Which one?" he finally asked.

I stepped in front of him to try and block Daniel's obviousness. I tilted my head over my shoulder slightly in the direction I wanted Daniel to look and said, "That guy over there in the blue shirt...*don't stare*," I hissed out when Daniel craned his neck to get a better look at Bryan.

"You mean that douche staring at you like a fat guy would look at a piece of pie?" he mock whispered.

I smacked him in the back of the head. "You're really eloquent, you know that?" I took a quick glance over my shoulder and saw that Bryan was currently staring down at his phone then I turned back to Daniel. "You're an asshole. Bryan's not a douche. He's just a guy that had the wrong idea."

With that, I turned and walked away.

A few minutes later I returned to Bryan's table with his meal, hoping he'd just let me drop off his food and walk away. I wasn't so lucky.

I'd just turned to walk away when I felt his hand wrap around my wrist to stop me. "Taylor," he spoke, not letting go of my wrist. "I was hoping I could convince you to have dinner with me tonight." His smile seemed genuine but there was something off putting about how he was looking at me.

I jerked my arm but he didn't let go so I reached down and pried his fingers from around my wrist and took a step back. "I'm flattered Bryan but I have a boyfriend. I'm sorry."

Something ghosted across his face but he quickly masked it with a smile before I could tell what it was. "Oh, of course. I'm so sorry. I didn't mean to make you feel uncomfortable."

I felt a twinge of guilt at turning him down. I hated the idea of hurting anyone's feelings. "You didn't make me uncomfortable," I lied in an attempt to make him feel a little better. "Is there anything else I can get you?"

He shook his head, maintaining his smile the entire time. "I'm good, thank you."

I turned away and released a relieved breath when I caught Daniel smirking at me from his table. The look on his face said clear as day "I told you so" and all it did was make me want to punch him.

"*Spit in your food*," I mouthed at him then laughed when the smiled instantly dropped from his face.

///.

Never seek to tell thy love,

Love that never told can be;

For the gentle wind doth move

Silently, invisibly.

I told me love, I told my love,

I told her all my heart,

Trembling, cold, in ghastly fears.

Ah! she did depart!

Soon after she was gone from me,

A traveler came by,

Silently, invisibly:

He took her with a sigh.

"Wake up, sweetheart."

Whose voice is that? I recognize it but I'm not sure from where.

"Come on, beautiful, wake up for me."

My eyes flitter open but the room is too dark to see anything. I placed my hands at my sides and try to push myself up into sitting position. There are no restraints keeping me in place but my head is foggy and the movement makes my stomach roll. The mattress I'm lying on feels dingy and one of the coils has poked through, jabbing me in the hip as my weight shifts.

I know this place.

I've seen it before but I'm having trouble focusing through the dizziness and nausea.

"I knew you were the one for me the second I saw you. You have the same haunted look in your eyes that I see every time I look in the mirror."

The man keeps talking in a low, monotone voice, and with each word, the nausea plaguing me gets worse. "I'm going to be sick."

The bile rises up, burning my throat and there is no holding it back. I lean to the side as my stomach empties its contents. As I wretch, the man rubs my hair and whispers soothing words. His touch causes the dry heaving to continue even though there is nothing left in my stomach. I wish he'd just leave me alone but I know that's not going to happen. I know I have to play his game and show no fear if I want a chance at surviving.

"Are you feeling better now, darling?" he asks, and I have to squeeze my eyes shut to keep the tears from falling.

"Yes, thank you. Could I please have some water?"

I can't see him but I feel his presence come closer, and when he speaks, his breath whispers over my skin. "Of course, my love. You can have anything you need. I'll always take care of you."

A whimper escapes me as his presses his lips to my cheek and I fight to hold back the tremors of disgust that fight to break free at his touch.

I feel the decrepit mattress shift as he lifts his weight from it and walks across the room. The sound of his shoes hitting the floor as he walks away echoes off the walls all around me.

I'm in a basement, I think to myself. I'm not sure how I know this but I have no doubt in my mind.

"It's just you and me until death," the man continues and I hear the sound of metal twisting seconds before its replaced by the sound of running water somewhere off to my right. "As soon as I deal with that pesky little problem of your boyfriend we can run away together. I swear to you; I'll make you happy."

Fear courses through me and I'm trembling so hard my teeth chatter. "What…what are you going to do to him?" I'm afraid of the answer but I have to know in case there's any way I can stop him.

He sits back down beside me and runs a hand down the side of my face. "He has to die. Please try to understand. If I let him live he'll come after you and try to take you away from me. I can't let that happen. I love you."

I break down in sobs and try desperately to reason with him, even though I know it's pointless. "Please, you don't have to do that," I plead. "Let's just go. We can leave now and run somewhere where he'll never find us. Just you and me…please. He probably won't even look for me."

"Are you still in love with him?" the man seethes. "Is that why you're crying and begging for his life?"

I scurry back on the mattress at the anger reverberating in his voice. "No," I whisper as tears run down. "I love you." I pray I'm able to convince him I'm telling the truth. "I'm so glad you got me away from him. I'm just scared of something happening to you if you get caught. He's a cop. How am I supposed to live if someone were to take you away from me?"

Saying these words is the hardest thing I've ever done and I hate myself for it, but I can't let him kill anyone else. I have to stop him.

"I love you," I choke out on a sob. I bite the inside of my cheek so hard the metallic taste of blood hits my tongue.

"I love you too," he rumbles and my heart speeds up to a dangerous level when I feel the mattress dip with his weight again. I don't know how long I can keep this up.

I cringe and turn my head away, thankful for the darkness when his fingers graze my jaw. I'm trying my hardest not to be consumed by the darkness around me when I hear something that both excites and terrifies me at the same time.

"TAYLOR!"

Oh, God. Oh, no! Please don't let him die.

"TAYLOR!"

I feel a crushing weight on my chest and the man pins me down on the filthy mattress. "You lying bitch," he hisses in my face. "You're just like the rest of them, you filthy whore. Now you get to watch as I kill your boyfriend. Then I'm going to kill you…slowly."

"No!" I scream at the top of my lungs just as a door bursts open and the room is flooded with light.

I catch a gleam of silver arcing through the air and scream at the top of my lungs. "JORDAN!"

His eyes go wide just as the knife plunges down.

My eyes popped open and my heart was beating so hard, I was afraid it would burst through my chest. I inhaled through my nose and out through my mouth, trying to calm myself when it finally dawned on me that Jordan hadn't woken up as I thrashed around from my nightmare. I shot my arm out to turn on the lamp on my bedside table and about collapsed when I turned to see the bed was empty.

I jumped up and ran to the bathroom hoping that he was in there. When I found it empty my heart plummeted. Tears burned my eyes and blurred my vision when a manic search of the apartment showed that Jordan was gone.

I had to find him.

I grabbed my phone to call him but my hands were shaking so badly, it took three tries to key his number in correctly.

"*Fuck!*" I screamed when his voicemail picked up. "Jordan, where are you? Call me as soon as you get this…*Please.*"

I disconnected the call and hit redial.

Voicemail again.

A strangled sob escaped my throat as I stood in my living room with my hands tugging the hair at my scalp in frustration. I was seconds away from a full blown panic attack when something caught my attention out of the corner of my eye.

I ran to the dining room table and snatched up the folded piece of paper.

Crimson,

Sorry I didn't wake you but you looked so peaceful and I didn't want to bother you. Had a break in the case so I'm heading to the station to check it out.

I'll call you later today. Love you, baby.

xx

-J

Shit. Dropping the letter to the floor, I bolted to my bedroom and threw on whatever clothes I grabbed first. I had to get to Jordan. I'd already lost Cassie; there was no way I was going to lose Jordan too. I couldn't handle another person I loved dying.

I'd just shoved my key in the deadbolt to lock the door when a noise behind me made me pause.

"Hello, beautiful."

I knew that voice. I recognized his cologne. Before I could turn to see who was behind me a cloth covered my mouth and nose. I didn't even have time to let out a scream before the acrid smell overwhelmed my senses and darkness enveloped me.

Jordan

This list of people who had installed commercial impact doors in their homes had come in early that morning. Even though the last thing I wanted to do was pull myself away from Taylor's soft, warm body that'd been wrapped around me like a blanket, I had to leave for the station to check it out. I needed to get this guy before he had the chance to hurt anyone else. Taylor had already lost so much at the hands of The Poet. I couldn't let her lose anyone else.

Stevens and I spent several hours running background checks on each of the names on that list and had come up with jack shit. The frustration was nagging at me and the dull throb of an impending headache pounded at the back of my eyes.

There was something there. I knew it, but I couldn't *see* it. I felt like the answer was staring me in the face and I couldn't figure it out.

"We need a break," Stevens exclaimed. "I feel like I'm going cross eyed."

I sat back in my chair and rubbed at my tired eyes. "Yeah, man. You're right."

He stood from the desk and stretched, straining the buttons on his shirt to their breaking point. "I'll grab us some lunch from Benny's. Be back in a few."

I waved my hand distractedly. "Sounds good." I was so fixated on finding The Poet that I couldn't concentrate on much else.

Once Stevens left, I pulled out my cell to call Taylor, needing to hear her voice to calm myself and clear my head. She was the only one who could help me do that.

"Damn it," I muttered when I realized that the battery had died some time that morning. I plugged it in to charge just as someone came running up to my desk.

"Jordan…" I turned to see Daniel breathing heavily like he'd run all the way to the station. "Something's wrong."

I shot out of my chair, sending it scraping across the floor with a loud screech. "Taylor?" was all I asked.

He nodded his head before shoving both hands through his already disheveled hair. When he didn't say anything else I grabbed him by the collar of his shirt and jerked him so close we were practically nose to nose. "What is it? What's happened?"

He started shaking his head manically, mumbling, "I don't know. I don't know," over and over. "Something's not right."

"What's not right, Daniel? I need fucking details!"

"It's a feeling…I know it sounds crazy, but I've got this gut feeling that she's in trouble. I tried calling her but she's not answering her phone. I went by the diner and Benny said she didn't show up for her shift so I came straight here since it was closer. I didn't know what the fuck else to do."

I'd never seen him so out of sorts and I'd learned enough in my time with Taylor to know not to dismiss a gut instinct. If Daniel felt something was wrong then something was *definitely* wrong.

Just then my cell phone pinged, alerting me to a new voicemail. I snatched the phone from its charger and hit the button to listen. When Taylor's scared voice came through the line the blood running through my veins turned to ice and the breath left my lungs.

"Jordan, where are you? Call me as soon as you get this…*Please.*"

I grabbed my keys and bolted for the door just as Stevens came walking through. "What's going on?" he asked as soon as he saw the look on my face.

I didn't stop walking as I called out, "It's Taylor. I've got to go. I'll call you as soon as I hear something."

I ran full speed to my car in the parking lot and turned it on as the passenger door flew open. "I'm coming with you," Daniel demanded. I didn't have time to argue, I just needed to get to Taylor.

The few minutes it took to get to her apartment building were the worst minutes of my life. Daniel and I burst through the doors like the devil was on our heels. I made a bee line for the elevators and pounded the button in rapid succession while Daniel headed over to Gary. I didn't know what he was saying to the old man but I didn't give a shit. I just needed to get up to her apartment.

I jumped into the elevator before the doors had a chance to open all the way. Each second it took to reach her floor took a year off my life.

Please let her be asleep. Please let her be asleep, I chanted to myself.

But as soon as the doors opened onto her floor I knew my prayers weren't going to be answered. The door to Taylor's apartment stood open and her keys hung out of the deadbolt. I rushed over and shoved it the rest of the way open, stepping over her purse and its spilled contents along the way. She wasn't answering her phone because she didn't have it. It was lying on the floor of the hall with the rest of her belongings.

"Taylor," I called out, already knowing I wasn't going to get an answer but trying anyway. I ran through the apartment, quickly discovering it was empty then rushed back downstairs to the lobby. The only thought running through my mind was that I couldn't lose her.

I ran to Gary, ignoring the tears in the old man's eyes and started throwing questions at him. "Who'd you let up to Taylor's apartment this morning?" I asked through clenched teeth.

"N…no one, Mr. Donovan."

"Bullshit! Someone has Taylor and they couldn't have gotten to her without going through you first. Now who the fuck did you let up?"

Gary looked like he was seconds away from a heart attack but I couldn't find it in myself to care.

"I swear! No one's even been by asking for her. I haven't seen anyone but the residents and…" His voice trailed off and his eyes grew wide.

"What is it?" Daniel asked. "Who else has been here?"

Gary's eyes darted back and forth between me and Daniel. "There are workers painting and installing new tile on the ninth floor but they don't come through me. They use the freight elevator to come and go."

"I need a list of every crew member that's working on those units. *Now!*"

As Gary clicked away at the computer on his desk, I started pacing back and forth.

"Jordan," Daniel called out, stopping me mid stride. "I don't know if it's related at all, but there was a guy in the diner the other day." The hairs on the back of my neck stood on end as a chill ran through me. "Taylor tried to brush it off as just some guy with a crush but she…*Christ*, I don't know…she seemed a little freaked out."

It was like a light bulb went off over my head as the memory came back to me. "Was the guy's name Bryan?"

"Yeah! Yeah, it was Bryan."

I stopped listening to what he was saying and pulled my phone from my pocket. "Stevens," I said as soon as the call connected. "Was there a guy named Bryan on that list?"

"Hold on, let me check." The sound of papers rustling came through before he spoke again. "Yeah, it's right here. Bryan Ackerman."

I ran behind Gary's desk and scanned through the list of names he'd printed off for me. Just as I suspected, there wasn't a Bryan anywhere on that list. He'd been stalking Taylor and snuck in with the crew working construction on the ninth floor. Gary hadn't seen him because he'd gone through the freight elevator. I grabbed a pen and spoke to Stevens, "Give me his address." I scribbled it down as he rattled it off.

"What's going on, man? Is Taylor okay?"

I was already heading out the door, leaving Daniel and Gary behind. "I'm ten minutes out. Call it in and get as many cars as you can over to Ackerman's. I think this guy's The Poet."

It wasn't an assumption. I knew it in my gut that we had found our guy.

"No shit?" Stevens asked.

"No shit. And he's got Taylor."

Taylor

"Wake up, sweetheart."

I came to feeling groggy and weak but my senses were in tune enough that even in the darkness I knew exactly what was happening. And I had to make sure the outcome was different from the one I'd seen in my nightmare. I wasn't going to let anything happen to Jordan.

"Come on, beautiful, wake up for me."

I shook my head, trying to wipe away some of the haziness and took a fortifying breath of damp air to try and prepare myself for the hell I was about to have to endure.

"Bryan, where are you? I can't see anything."

The mattress dipping down let me know he was close. "I'm right here, love. Don't worry, you're safe."

Keeping up the act was making me physically ill, but if it was what it took to save Jordan then I'd do it. I'd do anything for him. "Oh, thank God. I thought you'd left me alone. Can you turn on a light so I can see you?"

"Of course, anything for you."

I heard him moving around and sucked in a deep breath to stem off the waves of nausea I was experiencing. I heard a brief click then the room was illuminated in an eerie yellow light. I looked around at my surroundings trying to find anything that would help me. Gray concrete surrounded me on the floor and all four walls. The room didn't have a single window anywhere. The only way in or out was through the steel door that I'd seen in my vision. In the far right corner of the room there was a filthy, rust stained sink that had definitely seen better days. The only furniture in the cold room was the disgusting mattress that I was laying on and a small bedside table with a shade-less lamp sitting on top of it.

Next to the lamp sat a book that had clearly been read dozens of times. The spine was worn and cracked and it looked like some of the pages had been torn out. I blinked past the fuzziness that still affected my vision and took a closer look. It was a book of poetry. I could only guess that that was the book he'd torn poems from and placed in the hands of each of his victims.

The sight of it sent a shiver down my spine but I tried my best to mask it. "Where are we?"

Bryan reached up to tuck a strand of hair behind my ear and it took an enormous effort to keep myself from cringing at his touch. "I know you're probably scared right now, but you're safe. I promise. I'm so sorry if I frightened you."

I forced my lips up into a smile that I hoped looked sincere. "You didn't frighten me," I lied through my teeth. "I'm just so glad you found me."

"I knew you were the one for me the second I saw you. You have the same haunted look in your eyes that I see every time I look in the mirror." My body locked at those familiar words. They were the same words from my dream. "You're not like the others. They tricked me." His expression grew dark and angry as he spoke about his past victims. "They lied to make me believe they were something they weren't but in the end they were all the same…disgusting whores. Every woman in my life has disappointed me." The anger quickly morphed into something else and he looked at me with a loving smile. I was repulsed. "But you're different. I know I can trust you. When I saw you talking to that filthy slut from the diner I felt an instant connection."

Hearing him talk about Cassie in such a despicable way made me hate him even more. I wanted to reach over and claw his eyes out. The need to cause him immense pain was almost too much to handle.

"You had a sadness that I recognized because it's a part of me as well. The sorrow just makes your beauty stand out even more. You're the type of woman poems are written about."

This man was beyond insane. Just being in his presence disgusted me...but I had to push forward.

I reached my hand out and placed it on top of his and tried my best to ignore the creepy sensation I felt when our skin made contact. "Of course I'm not like them, Bryan. You and I are meant to be together. We're soul mates."

"Soul mates," he whispered in awe.

I told myself that if I could just keep the act up a little longer I could get us out of here and he wouldn't have the chance to hurt Jordan. I schooled my features in an attempt to look serious. "We have to get out of here. Jordan's probably looking for me and I don't want him to find us and take me away from you. We need to leave now."

The desperation in my voice was for Jordan's sake and luckily Bryan misinterpreted. "You don't need to worry, sweetheart. I'll never let him take you away from me again."

I stood from the mattress and tried to pull Bryan up with me. I had no clue what I was going to do once I got us out of wherever he was keeping me. Right then, I couldn't allow myself to think that far ahead. "Then let's go. We can leave now and he'll never find us. It'll be just you and me for the rest of our lives."

Bryan stood to his full height and pulled me into a tight embrace. The smell of his cologne might have been pleasing on anyone else but on him it just made me sick. "We can't leave yet, my love."

I was quickly growing to hate that endearment.

"I can't risk him tracking us down and taking you away. He has to die." He seemed so sincere as he spoke. A wave of terror wracked my body, and if he hadn't been holding me, my knees would have buckled.

"Bryan." My voice came out weak and pleading. "You don't have to kill anyone else. You've found me. There's no reason for anyone else to die. Jordan won't look for me once we're gone. I promise. It's just you and me forever."

"Until death," he spoke softly as he trailed a finger down my cheek. "Tell me that you love me," he demanded.

I swallowed past the sudden wave of nausea and looked up at him adoringly. "I love you."

Everything that was happening was too close to how it'd played out in my vision. I'd played along and acted the part in the hopes of changing the outcome but it had all been for nothing. He cupped my face in his hands and bent to press his lips to mine. I couldn't stop the tear that slipped down. "Don't you understand? I'm doing this for us. We'll never be able to be happy if we're constantly running."

I opened my mouth to speak again, but before I could get a word out, a loud crashing sound came from above, followed by the sound of Jordan bellowing my name.

The realization that I was too late washed over me, crippling me where I stood.

"You lying bitch," Bryan hissed at me as he backhanded me with so much force I went flying across the mattress. I placed both hands over my aching cheek and struggled to get back on my feet. "You're just like the rest of them, you filthy whore."

I heard Jordan yell my name again and I knew what was going to happen next. Seconds before the steel door burst open, Bryan pulled an eight inch hunting knife from the back of his jeans. I reacted purely on instinct when Jordan's figure came into sight and Bryan lunged for him.

"Jordan, get down!" I screamed as I threw myself between him and Bryan just as the knife sliced through the air.

"Taylor, no!"

Searing hot pain radiated through my chest as the air was pulled from my lungs. I fought to gasp for breath, but there was no use. The sound of gunshots reverberated off the walls followed by yelling. The last thing I remembered was seeing Jordan's face hovering above me. He had tears in his eyes but he was alive. I'd managed to save him and that was all that mattered. His life was all I cared about.

"You're safe," I whispered with a smile just before everything faded to black.

I was standing in my childhood bedroom and noticed that it looked the exact same way as it had when I was just a little girl.

"I told you that you were stronger than you knew," a voice said from behind me.

I spun around and gasped when I saw who was standing behind me. "Granny?" She looked exactly as she had the evening before my seventh birthday.

"I'm so proud of you, my sweet Lydia." She walked toward me and reached her hand out to brush her fingers over the locket she'd given to me years ago. "I never doubted that you'd do the right thing."

I single tears slid down my cheek at her declaration. "What are you talking about?"

"You saved that young man's life."

I knew exactly who she was talking about. Relief flooded me and I smiled at the knowledge that Jordan was okay. "You love him very much, don't you, sweet girl?"

I nodded as more tears flowed. "I do. He's the only man I've ever loved."

Granny smiled and her eyes glistened with unshed tears. "He loves you too, Lydia. You're so lucky to have a man who loves you as strongly and as passionately as he does. That's all I ever wanted for you, darling." As she spoke, her tears broke free and I reached to wipe them away. Granny grabbed hold of my hand and wrapped it in both of hers. "Hold on to that and never let it go."

"I won't, Granny, I promise."

She released my hand before cupping my cheeks and placing a soft kiss on my forehead. Then she placed one hand on my stomach and graced me with a beautiful, bright smile.

"With the love both you and your young man will give her she'll never have to live in fear."

At her words, I let out a sob and covered my mouth with both hands. "You teach her well, my precious Lydia. Stand by her and show that she has nothing to fear. You can be there for her in all the ways I wish I could have been there for you."

I nodded my head and both of our tears ran freely as I placed my hands over my grandmother's. "I will. I love you, Granny."

"I love you too, darling."

My eyes fluttered open but the light in the room made the pounding in my head so much worse. "Too bright," I croaked. My throat felt dry and scratchy and I hardly recognized my voice.

"Oh thank Christ. She's awake!" I heard a deep voice declare way too loudly.

"I'll get Jordan," another, somewhat raspy female voice exclaimed.

I heard shuffling around the room and the lights thankfully dimmed slightly so I was finally able to open my eyes all the way. Daniel was hovering directly over me, so close I could see my reflection in his crystal blue eyes.

"How are you feeling?" he asked.

I let out a groan as the sound of his voice banged around inside my head. "I'd be a lot better if you'd back the hell up. Jesus, I can tell you had onions for lunch."

Daniel shot up and called over his shoulder seriously, "She's going to be just fine. The knife didn't sever the sarcastic artery."

Seconds later, he went flying out of my line of sight and I heard the sounds of a scuffle going on in the corner of the room. "Is there ever a time of day or night when you aren't a complete douche hole?" My heart rate picked up at the sound of Jordan's voice. I tried to turn my head to look at him, but even that slight movement sent pain shooting through me.

"Probably not," Daniel replied casually.

"Jordan," I cried desperately.

Instantly, he was standing over me and the sight of his tired, smiling face brought tears to my eyes. "I thought he was going to kill you," I sobbed.

He ran a hand softly over my head as he made soothing sounds in my ear. "It's okay, Crimson. Don't cry. I'm right here. I'm okay, everyone's okay."

"I see our patient's finally awake," An older, deep voice called from the doorway of the room. I tried to push up but a sharp, shooting pain sliced through my chest causing me to lose my breath. "Slow down, sweetheart," the older man said as he walked over to my bedside. He fiddled with a few buttons on the side of my bed and I was slowly raised to sitting position in the bed. My eyes took in everyone standing in the room. The first thing I noticed was Benny standing over in the corner of the room, her eyes red as tears streamed down her face.

Gary stood at her side with a comforting arm wrapped tightly around her shoulder. The look on his face was a combination of sadness and gratitude.

Jordan was standing to my right holding my hand firmly in both of his and Daniel stood behind an older man to my left. He was wearing a white lab coat and I could only assume he was my doctor. His handsome features were highlighted by a thick head of dark hair with a smattering of gray around his temples. The best word to describe him was distinguished. If I went for older men—and if I wasn't completely and utterly in love with Jordan—I might have been tempted to make a play for the silver fox.

Sensing my appreciation of the handsome doctor, Jordan gave my hand a squeeze, pulling my attention to his dark, slightly irritated eyes. "You've been awake for all of thirty seconds after scaring ten years off my life. You think you could refrain from giving the doc here come hither eyes?"

My blush came back full force, warming my cheeks to a feverish level. "Sorry, baby," I muttered. "I love you."

He leaned over to me and planted a closed mouth, possessive kiss on my lips. "Love you too, Crimson."

A chuckle to my left pulled me out of my lust filled haze and caused the redness on my cheeks to darken even more. "I'm Dr. Andrews, it's nice to finally meet you. I think I can speak for all of us when I say we're very happy you're finally awake, Ms. Carmichael. You've given your friends here quite a scare."

My mind flashed with images of the last thing I remembered and I started to feel the telltale signs of a panic attack starting, setting off the monitors behind my head. Dr. Andrews stepped over and started pushing some buttons to silence the annoying beeping. "Try and calm down, Ms. Carmichael, you're safe now. Nothing is going to happen to you here. I need you to try and relax and calm your breathing."

I sucked in a deep breath and instantly regretted it as that pain ripped through my chest again. My eyes shot down to the white bandage that started at my collar bone on my right side and extended down to the center of my chest. "What happened?" I finally managed to ask.

"Ms. Carmichael, do you remember what happened to you?" I felt tears clogging my throat and couldn't speak past them so I just nodded. "You were stabbed. And I have to say, you were extremely lucky. Other than severe blood loss and a pretty nasty knife wound, you didn't sustain any serious internal injuries. We were able to repair the damage and control the bleeding. The surgery took about two hours and you've been unconscious since yesterday."

As the doctor spoke my grandmother's words echoed in my head. "The baby?" I asked, almost scared to hear his answer.

Dr. Andrews' hand reached for the hospital blanket that was covering my stomach and pulled it back to reveal a round contraption, held together with an elastic band that wrapped around my abdomen resting on the center of my belly. "This is a fetal monitor Ms. Carmichael. If you look at that monitor right there you'll see that the baby's heart rate is just fine."

My tears broke free and I cried in relief that the baby I didn't even know existed until just a few minutes before was doing just fine. I turned to my right to see Jordan's reaction. He'd already had a day to come to grips with the fact that he was going to be a father, but that didn't mean he was necessarily going to be happy about it.

All of the anxiety I felt at the thought of Jordan not wanting this instantly disappeared as I watched the biggest, brightest grin spread across his face when the doctor talked about our baby.

"The obstetrician will be in later today to speak with you, but so far your little one is a fighter just like its mommy."

After the doctor checked my vitals and examined the staples he'd used on my wound, he announced that everything was healing beautifully and depending on what the obstetrician said, I should be able to go home in the next few days.

Benny and Gary both hung around for a few minutes after Dr. Andrews left to hug and cry over me. By the time the two of them left I was completely exhausted and in more than a little bit of pain, but I had questions that I needed answers to.

"What happened with Bryan?" I finally asked once only Daniel and Jordan were left in the room with me.

Daniel dropped his head but I noticed his eyes grew shiny before he looked down to study his shoes. Seeing the tears in his eyes hurt my heart and almost set me off again.

Jordan cleared his throat and scratched the back of his neck uncomfortably before looking back at me. "He's dead, baby."

I recalled hearing a gunshot right before I passed out. "You shot him, didn't you?"

Daniel dropped into the chair beside me and Jordan rested on the bed next to me and reached for my hand. "When you dove in front of me and I saw that knife…" His voice cracked and a single tear escaped his eyes. "I thought I'd lost you. You hit the ground and I just fired."

I took as deep a breath as I could without hurting my chest. "So it's over? We don't have to worry about him anymore?" It almost seemed too good to be true.

"It's over, baby," Jordan said quietly.

He leaned in and squeezed me as tightly as he could without hurting me and we just held each other for several minutes.

"We're going to have a baby," he whispered in awe after pulling back slightly to look in my eyes.

I smiled at Jordan with so much love inside me it was overwhelming. After several seconds the sound of a clearing throat pulled us back into reality.

Daniel smiled sheepishly and in that moment, I knew he knew. "Daniel," I whispered. I didn't need to say anything else.

"I know, honey. It's going to be okay. I promise."

Jordan's eyes darted back and forth between me and Daniel. "Someone want to tell me what's going on?"

I took Jordan's hand in mine and placed it on my belly. "I saw my grandmother," I stated. "I don't know if it was a dream or a vision but... I saw her. That's how I knew I was pregnant." I smiled again as tears streamed down my cheek. "It's a little girl, Jordan."

His jaw dropped and his eyes bugged out. "A girl?"

I nodded.

"I'm going to have a baby girl?" His dimples popped as the realization hit him and the joy I saw on his face was contagious.

"Baby, I have to tell you something," I finally said, hating to burst our happy little bubble.

"What? What's the matter? Is something wrong with her?" he asked worriedly.

I looked at Daniel at a loss as to how to explain it to Jordan. Daniel took pity on me and dropped the bomb himself. "She's going to be a Seer, Jordan. She's going to have the same gift her mother and her great-grandmother did."

"Wait…" Jordan shook his head violently. "No. No! I won't let my little girl go through what Taylor suffered with all her life. I won't!"

I grabbed his face in my hands, feeling a sense of calm that I'd never experienced before. "Do you trust me?" I asked.

He didn't speak, only nodded.

"Then you have to believe me when I tell you that our little girl is going to be just fine. With the love that you and I are going to give her, she's never going to have to grow up in fear the way I did. I have faith in that. I need you to as well." I ran my thumb along his lower lip gently before asking, "Do you believe me?"

Jordan turned his face into my palm and planted a loving kiss in the center. "I do, Crimson." We smiled at each other before something crossed over his face. "Wait a minute." He turned and addressed Daniel. "You said she was going to have the same gift her mother and grandmother *had*."

It was Daniel's turn to clear his throat uncomfortably. "Yeah, well…you know that higher power I was talking about?"

Jordan and I both nodded in the affirmative.

"An exception was made for Taylor. It's never been done before…but…well, you were never supposed to come so close to dying, Taylor. After everything…everything you've suffered through in your life, a decision was made. You can choose to relinquish your gift and live the rest of your life like you've always wanted to." He smiled but there was a sadness in his eyes.

I was shocked. I don't know how long I sat there, just staring at Daniel. "I have a choice?"

"You do."

I didn't know what to think. Then the reason for his sadness hit me. "What about you? If I'm no longer a Seer will I still get to see you?"

He shook his head and the sadness radiating off him filled the room. "If you aren't a Seer there's no reason for you to have a Guide."

I looked back at Jordan and saw understanding reflected back at me. He knew how important Daniel was to me because he had grown to be important to Jordan also. "But you're my family," I told Daniel. "I've finally accepted my gift; I'm not scared of it anymore. If giving it up means I lose you too then I'm keeping it."

I don't think I could have said anything that would have surprised him more. "Taylor, this is what you've wanted your whole life; a chance to be normal and to build a family without this hanging over your head. This is a lot to take in. You need to at least give it some thought. Don't jump to a decision right now."

I reached down and caressed my belly. "There's nothing to think about," I replied. "I've already built my family and you're a part of it."

Daniel's eyes brightened and he let out a cough to mask the tears that were threatening to fall. Jordan released my hand and stood to walk around the bed. He lifted his hand for Daniel to shake and gave him a sincere smile. "Welcome to the family, Uncle Daniel."

7 ½ Years Later

"Cassandra Marilyn Donovan, I told you to clean your room or I was going to cancel your birthday party tomorrow," I called from the hall as I made my way toward the living room.

"But Moooom," she whined to me from her seat on the couch between her father and uncle. "It's the bottom of the ninth. I can't leave now. The Mariners are about the kick White Sox ass."

Jordan choked on the drink of beer he'd just taken and Daniel let out a bark of laughter. I narrowed my eyes at my little girl and demanded, "Room. Now. Or I'm calling Benny to cancel your princess cake, and telling Gary not to let any of your friends up for your party."

Cassie let out an exasperated huff and headed toward her bedroom, moping the whole way. I watched as my beautiful, hazel eyed little girl walked out of the room before turning back to the two most important men in my life. "You're horrible influences. You know that, right?"

"It was him!" Daniel insisted like a kid caught with his hand caught in a candy jar. "I told him to watch his mouth in front of the kid."

"Oh, bullshit!" Jordan demanded. "You're just as bad as I am. You just called me a douche nozzle in front of *the kid*."

I rolled my eyes at the both of them. It had been like this for the past eight years. "Can you please refrain from calling my daughter *the kid*, please?"

Jordan grabbed me by my hips and pulled me down into his lap. "Have I mentioned how in love with you I am?" he asked, trying to win brownie points.

"Hmm." I tapped my chin and squinted at the ceiling. "Not today."

He shot me that dimpled grin before giving me a lingering kiss. "I love you, baby."

"I love you, too."

Daniel let out a gagging sound next to us. "It's times like these I wish you *would* have relinquished your gift. This lovey dovey shit makes me itchy."

"Hey," Jordan stated. "You're the one who told me that we were meant to find each other."

"Yeah, but I didn't think I'd be stuck seeing you suck face on a regular basis. I was hoping she'd friend-zone your ass so I wouldn't have to deal with this shit."

Jordan reached over and punched Daniel in the arm. "Sorry, buddy boy. Fate made its decision a long time ago. Deal with it.

⁙⁙⁙⁙⁙⁙⁙⁙⁙⁙⁙⁙⁙⁙⁙⁙⁙⁙⁙⁙⁙⁙⁙⁙⁙⁙⁙⁙⁙⁙⁙⁙.

Cassie had taken her bath and was lying in her bed after I finished reading her a bedtime story. Jordan and Daniel joined me at her bedside to have the most important conversation we'd ever have with her.

"Do you have any clue how special you are, my sweet Cassie?" I asked as I clasped my grandmother's locket around her tiny neck. "You're just like me, love. We have a special gift."

It was the night before my daughter's seventh birthday.

Cassie knew she was special. We'd never hidden it from her, but until tonight, she didn't know the extent of her gift.

"What special gift, Mommy?" she asked, staring at me with those gorgeous eyes she'd inherited from her dad. Her head was in my lap as I ran my fingers through her light brown hair just like my grandmother had for me when I was her age.

"We can see things, sweet girl. Special things that no one else can see. We have visions," I whispered with a smile, repeating the same words my grandmother said to me so many years ago. "And it's our job to try and help the people we see in our visions."

Cassie's bottom lip trembled and Jordan and Daniel stepped closer in a show of support. "I'm scared," she whispered in a small voice that broke my heart.

"Do you remember where you got your name from, baby girl?" I asked her.

"Yeah. You named me Cassandra after your best friend and Marilyn after your Granny."

I stroked her hair lovingly. "That's right. I named you after the two strongest people in the whole entire world. You know why I did that?"

She shook her head and looked up at me inquisitively.

"Because you're just as strong as they are," I whispered. "You just don't know it yet."

She ran her finger over the locket I'd passed on to her lightly before wrapping her fingers around it and holding on tight.

"And you have me, Daddy and Uncle Daniel and we're always going to be here for you."

"So I'm going to see the things like you do?"

"That's right, baby," Jordan said. "Your Mommy helps people and now you're going to get to help people too."

That got a beautiful, dimpled smile from my precious girl...my angel. "Like a super hero? I'm gonna get to save people like you and Mommy?"

Jordan chuckled before planting a kiss on Cassie's forehead. "Just like a superhero, Angel."

"And Uncle Daniel's gonna help me too?"

All those years ago I'd made the decision to hold on to my gift when I had the chance to let it go and lead a normal life. Other than allowing myself to fall in love with, and marry Jordan, it was the best decision I ever made. Daniel was my Guide, my friend...my family. And because I accepted my gift, I got something special in return. Daniel was going to be Cassie's Guide. He was going to be with her for the rest of her life, protecting her and loving her.

"Yeah, sweetheart, I'm going to be there to help you too."

I looked at my daughter then back to Jordan and Daniel. "Some of the things you see may frighten you but you have to be strong. We'll always be there to protect you. Me, Daddy and Uncle Daniel will never ever let anything hurt you."

"Okay, Mommy."

Cassie was so trusting and brave; my heart swelled with pride as I looked down at her. I knew she was going to be just fine. I'd named her properly.

She was so much stronger than she even knew.

I stepped back so that Daniel and Jordan could kiss her good night and as I stood leaning against the doorway, looking at the three most important people in my life, I soaked up the love that filled the room.

The vision in front of me was the one I'd always wanted. It was my family. I'd finally embraced my gift, and in doing so, I'd allowed myself to accept the love that Jordan had given me.

My life was full of light.

The darkness was finally gone and I knew without a doubt that there was nothing but brightness ahead of me.

Acknowledgments

The very first person I want to acknowledge is my wonderful husband. Thank you so much for putting up with me checking out for extended periods of time in order to write. You are the best husband a woman could ask for and an amazing father to our son. I love you so much.

To my family, I couldn't do this without all the love and support I get from each and every one of you. I have the best support system in the world.

To my dear friends Lynda Ybarra and Lisa Chamberlin, thank you so much for putting up with endless texting and voxxing. You read Nightmares from Within from the very beginning and helped make it into something that I love even more. I'm proud to call the two of you friends.

To Sandra Cortez for being a kickass beta reader, a great friend, and my go to on what's trendy.

Lastly, I have to say thank you to my readers. I wouldn't be anywhere if it weren't for y'all. Thank you so much for taking a chance on me.